THE GHOST CADET

CADET
W.H. McDOWELL
BORN IN
NORTH CAROLINA
DEC. — 1846.
Private Co. B Corps
of Cadets.
KILLED MAY 15, 1864,
AT BATTLE OF
NEW MARKET VA.

☆ T ☆ H ☆ E ☆

GHOST CADET

★ ★ ★ ★ ★ ★ ★ ★ ★ ★ ★

Elaine Marie Alphin

Henry Holt and Company

NEW · YORK

First edition
Published by Henry Holt and Company, Inc.,
115 West 18th Street, New York, New York 10011.
Published simultaneously in Canada by Fitzhenry & Whiteside Ltd.,
195 Allstate Parkway, Markham, Ontario L3R 4T8.

Library of Congress Cataloging-in-Publication Data
Alphin, Elaine Marie.
The ghost cadet / Elaine Marie Alphin.
Summary: Twelve-year-old Benjy, in Virginia visiting the grandmother he has never met,
meets the ghost of a Virginia Military Institute cadet who was killed in the Battle of
New Market in 1864 and helps him recover his family's treasured gold watch.
ISBN 0-8050-1614-7
1. New Market, Battle of, 1864—Juvenile fiction. [1. New Market, Battle of, 1864—
Fiction. 2. United States—History—Civil War, 1861–1865—Campaigns—
Fiction. 3. Ghosts—Fiction. 4. Grandmothers—Fiction.] I. Title.
PZ7.A4625Gh 1991   90-24180
[Fic]—dc20

Henry Holt books are available at special discounts
for bulk purchases for sales promotions, premiums,
fund-raising, or educational use. Special editions or
book excerpts can also be created to specification.

Printed in the United States of America
on acid-free paper. ∞
1 3 5 7 9 10 8 6 4 2

For Art,
who has always believed

☆ ☆ ☆

CONTENTS

☆ 1 ☆

THE SHAKING TREE

"**I** just can't believe she's done this to me!"

Benjy Stark squeezed himself closer to the window and tried to ignore his sister's complaints. He knew Fran wasn't really talking to him. She never bothered with him anymore if she could help it.

"I mean, it's my vacation," Fran went on. For the dozenth time since their mother had put them on the Greyhound bus early that morning, Fran shifted angrily around in her creaking seat, trying to get comfortable. "Why do I have to spend it buried off in the country just so she can have some time to herself? I had plans for this spring break—I had a lot of things to do with my friends."

Benjy stared hard through the window and tuned his sister out. It was his vacation too, wasn't it? And no one had asked him if he wanted to spend it in Virginia with a grandmother he didn't even know. Not that it had happened exactly the way Fran said, of course.

Benjy sometimes thought his sixteen-year-old sister re-arranged her memories to suit the role she wanted to see herself playing. In reality, their mother hadn't been completely comfortable about the plan herself.

"Your grandmother has wanted to meet you two for so long," she'd tried to explain.

"I'll bet," Fran had muttered.

"This seems like such a good time," Mrs. Stark struggled on.

"For you," Fran told her.

"Yes."

Benjy remembered his mother had been up front enough about that.

"I need to get away myself. If I spend one more day in that office with my supervisor ranting on about how much work is backing up and the other girls complain-ing about their husbands—" She'd interrupted herself. "I just can't take it and take it and take it—I need a break. Andy can get some time off from work also, and we need this time together."

She'd looked back and forth from Fran to Benjy. "I hope you both know how important Andy is becoming to me. I'd like to think he is to you too."

Fran had groaned and rolled her eyes. Mrs. Stark had looked at Benjy, but he'd looked away. He hadn't wanted to think about Andy and his mother. He didn't want to think about it now.

And anyway, being sent to Virginia didn't make any

difference to him. He never had any plans for the holidays. Spring break was just a good excuse to stay away from the kids who picked on him at school. Well, Benjy told himself, Virginia was a long way away from the other kids. Maybe it wouldn't be such a bad vacation after all.

As the bus rushed down Interstate 81, Benjy studied the rolling countryside. He was glad he'd taken a good look at the big atlas in the school library before the vacation started. At least he had some idea of where they were. Their grandmother lived in a little town called New Market, in the Shenandoah Valley. New Market was about midway between Winchester and Lexington. Benjy remembered there were all kinds of historical places in Lexington, like Washington and Lee University and the Virginia Military Institute. Lexington might be worth going to see.

Benjy told himself not to count on it. Probably their grandmother wouldn't be interested in showing them the sights. He sighed and concentrated on the view through the window. On his right as they rumbled through the valley, Benjy could see the mighty Allegheny Mountains rising up in the distance. A second, smaller road chased the interstate, winding patiently around the natural curves of the valley while the faster road plowed straight ahead.

On Benjy's left the Blue Ridge Mountains formed the other side of the valley. But in front of them the

Massanutten, an odd-shaped mountain, stood guard over the Shenandoah. Benjy thought it looked like a huge dog, drowsing on its side in the afternoon sun. The dog's head looked to the east, out of the valley, and the mountain seemed to shrink away into the dog's tail, pointing deep into the valley's heart. Benjy smiled to himself, half expecting the dog to stand up, give itself a good shake, and trot away.

He jumped as his sister punched his arm without warning.

"And a big help you were," Fran was saying angrily. "You could have said something to her, told her you wouldn't go or something, instead of leaving me to try and talk her out of it all by myself."

Benjy rubbed his arm and looked at Fran cautiously. He knew she was furious, but he couldn't see what she'd expected him to do about it. The trip had been their mother's idea, not his.

"Tell you what," Fran said slyly. "There is one thing you could do, Benjy."

"What?" he asked suspiciously. He could hear the fake sweetness in her voice and had a feeling she was up to something.

"When we get there," Fran said, "I'm going to tell that old lady I won't stay and I'm going to make her send us home. What I want you to do is back me up— okay, Benjy?"

"How?" If it was something easy and he did a good

job, maybe Fran would be pleased with him. She might even want to do things with him again once they got home. When they'd been younger, Fran had played with him a lot. She always had zany ideas and she'd make up all kinds of games just for the two of them, and they'd laugh and laugh. But everything had changed. Since their father left, Fran never wanted anything to do with her family. First she found girl-friends her own age to laugh with, and now she had boyfriends. She never had time for Benjy anymore. But maybe this vacation would pull them together again. After all, neither of them knew anybody in New Market, even their grandmother. Benjy looked at her hopefully.

"You could throw one of those tantrums like you used to," Fran announced triumphantly. "Break some stuff and yell your head off, and the old lady'll be only too happy to get rid of us!"

A dark flush crept across Benjy's pale face. He started to shake his head.

"Come on, Benjy—I know you're getting too old for that now. I mean, twelve is a little too old for screaming and throwing stuff, isn't it? But you can fake it, can't you?" Underneath Fran's mocking voice, there was a half-pleading note.

Benjy tensed, clenching his fists. He hated the tantrums he had thrown when he was younger, and couldn't help having even now sometimes. Once it was all over, he hated himself. But people kept hammering at him—he'd get furious because he couldn't do anything about it, so he'd run away inside himself where they couldn't touch him, or explode with a tantrum. Afterward they usually left him alone.

But right then he wanted to throw a whale of a tantrum right there in the bus, just like Fran said. And what he'd like to break was his sister! She wasn't ever going to like him or be friends with him again, no matter what he did, and he was angry at himself for ever imagining she would.

"Forget it," he muttered. "I want to stay here for spring vacation."

"I bet you do," Fran snapped. "I bet you think it's just great staying with our grandmother—our father's mother, no less. It's not enough he just walked out on us and left us stuck with Mom; now we're getting dumped on his mother! I bet she's just thrilled to have us—and she's going to love you, Benjy Stark—you're starting to look more and more like he did. She's really going to love a grandson who looks just like her own no-good son!"

Sick inside, Benjy twisted away from his sister and glared at the window. He could see himself reflected dimly in the glass, a thin, pinched face under a shock of tangled blond hair. It was his father's face. Both Fran and their mother had black hair.

For a second, Benjy could almost see his father

again—his face aglow with elfin delight, his long, slender fingers weaving gracefully through the air as he talked, telling them some wonderful, absurd story he'd made up—Benjy had loved those best. But that had been years and years ago. Benjy's memory slammed shut, and all he saw were the empty years when no one had been there except his stupid sister, and a mother who was always busy, and the older kids in his class who laughed at him and called him a baby. It wasn't his fault the teachers had put him a grade ahead so he was always the youngest in his class, he thought resentfully. After his father left, Benjy spent more and more time reading and just got ahead of the kids his own age. And since he got put ahead a grade, he never fit in with any of his classmates. He didn't have anyone to teach him to play ball or wrestle or any of the things the other boys knew how to do. Everything had gone wrong after his father had walked out on them. The last person in the world Benjy wanted to look like was his lousy, deserting father!

In the window Benjy could see Fran's reflection, too. He'd sealed off his ears so he wouldn't have to listen to her, but she wasn't laughing any longer. Her face was bent down, the long dark hair half hiding it. If he didn't know her better, he'd guess she was crying.

Benjy shut out the thought. He wished he'd brought some books to read, but he couldn't check them out from the school library over vacation. Anyway, Fran would probably have spent the bus ride sneering at him for being a bookworm. So he forgot about reading and concentrated on looking through Fran's reflection at the rolling valley once again. It was a clear, still spring afternoon, and the countryside was thick with new green leaves and early flowers. Benjy couldn't believe how beautiful it was. There certainly wasn't anything like this open landscape in the city. There was a park in their neighborhood, but the grass was brown and patchy and the kids had torn the small branches off the trees as high as they could reach.

As he watched, they passed a neatly kept field. Trees hid parts of it from the interstate, but through them Benjy suddenly caught a glimpse of a cannon. He straightened up in his seat and caught sight of it again before it disappeared and he saw a small orchard and a two-story white house. Around the house was a collection of smaller stone and weathered board buildings surrounded by a white rail fence. In the distance, beyond the old-fashioned buildings, Benjy could see a large, flat, round building with several flags flying in front of it. Just past the large white house, a few more trees were scattered near two more small buildings. The deserted buildings looked peaceful, and the trees hung motionless in the still air. Then, as Benjy watched, one of the trees began to shake violently.

☆ 2 ☆

MISS LEOTA

Benjy was still wondering if he could have imagined the tree shaking all by itself, when the bus suddenly ground its gears and lurched onto an exit ramp. None of the other passengers seemed to have noticed the tree's stormy behavior. Benjy saw that they were all busy reading, napping, or talking to their neighbors. He didn't dare ask Fran if she'd seen anything. She'd only laugh at him again.

The bus swung heavily around under the interstate, passed a cluster of touristy-looking hotels and gift shops, and pulled jerkily up a short slope. The driver guided it through a turn at a narrow intersection, passed a three-story building with the names LEE and JACKSON prominently stenciled in gold on it, and shuddered to a stop in the parking lot of the Battlefield Restaurant.

"New Market!" the driver called out.

"Oh, no!" Fran moaned dramatically. But she got to

her feet and began collecting her carry-on luggage.

Benjy jumped up and grabbed his small nylon backpack, the strange tree already forgotten. He pushed
past Fran, eager to get away from her, while she
was still shoving her things into an immense canvas
carryall.

"Remember," Fran warned, poking him in the back.
"I'm getting out of this dump, and you're going to help
me."

Benjy ignored her. He swung his backpack over one
shoulder and started down the aisle.

Only two other people got off in New Market. They
were already collecting their luggage at the side of the
bus by the time Benjy climbed down the stairs and
stood looking around.

"Get a move on, will you?" Fran snapped, hurrying
down the steps and shoving past him. "Get your suitcase."

Benjy followed her to the luggage the bus driver was
unloading. In a moment Fran's large blue suitcase and
Benjy's smaller brown case were on the ground, and
the baggage compartment's door was slammed shut.
The driver climbed back into the bus and headed toward the interstate.

Benjy looked around uncertainly. The two people
who had gotten off first were already gone, and he
couldn't see anyone who looked as though she was
waiting to pick up two children she'd never seen.

"Maybe the bus got here early?" Benjy asked his sister.

"Maybe the old lady isn't too anxious to see us," Fran retorted, tossing her hair back. "Anyhow, I'm not going to stand around in this parking lot all day. I'll ask in that restaurant, if I can find anybody who knows anything in this crummy town."

Fran disappeared purposefully through the side door of the Battlefield Restaurant. Benjy looked up and down the street. All he could see were tiny shops and offices. He checked the street sign curiously. Congress Street. Benjy had a sinking feeling that this was the center of town. Everything looked weather-beaten and tired. Benjy wondered if his grandmother would be faded and tired, too.

He decided to join Fran in the restaurant. He swung his backpack into place and picked up his suitcase. Briefly he considered just leaving Fran's suitcase in the dusty parking lot, but decided the satisfaction probably wouldn't be worth the trouble it would cause. Sighing, he gripped the handle of Fran's heavy suitcase and dragged it awkwardly to the restaurant entrance. Fran was standing just inside the screen door, talking to a man in shirtsleeves.

"Mrs. Stark," Fran was saying. She sounded exasperated. "She's supposed to meet us—we're her grandchildren!"

"Miss Leota?" the man's voice drawled curiously.

"Well, now, I didn't know Miss Leota had grandchildren coming to visit. Young Edward's children, you must be. Miss Leota must be real pleased."

Yeah, thrilled, Benjy thought, feeling a surge of resentment rise up against his mother. He couldn't blame his grandmother. Her daughter-in-law just up and decided to go on a little holiday and shipped the kids off to their grandmother. If she couldn't be bothered to care about her own children, why should their grandmother be pleased to get them? He shut out the nagging voice in his head that said this wasn't quite fair to his mother.

"But where is she?" Fran persisted. "Was the bus early or something?"

"No," the man said cheerfully, "right on time. I expect Miss Leota'll be here any time now."

"Well, can we call her or something?" Fran asked impatiently.

Suddenly Benjy felt a pair of hands on his shoulders. He spun around and found himself staring at a slight woman wearing a crisp linen skirt and a soft gray turtleneck sweater. She was barely over five feet tall, and very slender, but from her grip on his shoulders Benjy knew she was anything but frail. Her face was a maze of fine wrinkles framed by white hair pulled neatly into a bun, and she was examining Benjy through a pair of remarkably clear blue eyes.

Benjy took an involuntary step back on the parking

lot blacktop. He recognized the high cheekbones and the thin face. It was so like his father's and yet so different—for a moment Benjy wanted desperately to run to her and bury himself in one of the huge bear hugs his father had always been ready with. But this face wasn't his father's; it was much stronger. Anyway, his father sure wasn't ready with any bear hugs these days. Why should this woman be? Benjy felt a hot fury inside his head. Why couldn't he blot out the memories?

Embarrassed at his unpredictable temper, Benjy took a deep breath and made his face go blank. Sometimes that worked to seal off the anger. At least, it usually fooled other people. He looked coolly at the person in front of him.

"Grandmother?" he asked, keeping his voice expressionless.

"Miss Leota!" the man called from inside the restaurant. "There now, young lady, didn't I say Miss Leota would be here?"

"Thank you, Charles," the lady called in an unexpectedly strong, clear voice. To Benjy, she said, "I believe I would prefer 'Miss Leota' to 'Grandmother.' Perhaps if I were not a widow and lived surrounded by my family I'd prefer 'Grandmother,' but that is not the case."

"I'm sorry," Benjy apologized, still trying to sound distant. Of course she didn't want to treat him like family. Why should she? Hadn't Fran said she wouldn't want him around reminding her of his father?

"Don't be," Miss Leota said briskly. Her face relaxed into a surprisingly warm smile. "How could you have known? You must be Benjamin."

Benjy nodded. He felt oddly ashamed of his tangled hair falling into his eyes and his faded blue jeans and denim jacket. Everything was clean, but his clothes were so old they were wearing thin. He felt shabby, and it embarrassed him. It made him angry, too. It wasn't his fault his mother didn't have the time to shop for clothes for him, or the money to buy new things when his old stuff wore out. Before he could think of anything to say to his grandmother, Fran burst out through the door, already talking.

"We just call him Benjy, Miss Leota, and I'm Fran. I wasn't sure if we should wait for you or go looking for your house or what."

Fran looked much better, Benjy thought. She was wearing a pair of fairly new black leggings and a loose, oversized rust-and-purple sweater. In the past couple of years she had started thinking a lot about clothes and had saved up baby-sitting money to get some nice things. But Benjy thought Miss Leota didn't look terribly impressed. Maybe he was wrong about his grandmother. Maybe she hadn't already made up her mind to dislike him and favor his sister. Maybe she just accepted people as they were.

"Yes. You're Frances," was all she said. "I have never been in the habit of hurrying, so I do occasionally arrive at my destination a bit late. There are few things that can't wait a minute or two." She smiled at the heavyset man standing in the restaurant doorway. "Thank you for reassuring them, Charles."

"No problem at all, Miss Leota," the man assured her. "Nice for you, having young Edward's children for a visit."

"Yes. We'll see," Miss Leota told him. "Thank you again, Charles. You have been most patient with them."

"My pleasure, Miss Leota," he said good-naturedly, "Bye now, kids!" he called before turning to go back inside.

Miss Leota stood still a moment, studying her two grandchildren. "Well," she said finally, "I expect after your long bus ride you would like to stretch your legs. My home is just a few blocks from here."

"What about our suitcases?" Fran exclaimed.

Benjy had already reached for his own suitcase, uncomfortably aware of his grandmother's scrutiny. When he looked up, he saw with relief that Miss Leota's attention had shifted to Fran and her heavy suitcase.

"I can't carry that," Fran stated flatly.

"How did you get it to the bus in the first place?" Miss Leota asked thoughtfully.

"Mom drove us," Fran told her. "Don't you have a car?"

"I do," Miss Leota said, "but this is such a pleasant day I chose to walk."

"Well, what am I supposed to do with this suitcase?" Fran demanded.

"It's entirely up to you," Miss Leota said, unruffled. "You can bring it with you now or leave it here with Mr. Mitchell until I have time to pick it up in the car later."

"When is later?" Fran asked quickly.

Miss Leota shrugged slightly. "Perhaps later this afternoon if the opportunity presents itself."

Benjy wanted to laugh. For once someone actually had his sister flustered! He felt a little nervous when Miss Leota fixed him with those direct blue eyes, but at the same time he was starting to like her. He hefted his own suitcase and grinned at no one in particular.

"What are you so tickled about?" his sister snapped. "Just because you didn't have anything to pack anyway—you could at least offer to help me."

"Frances, that will do," Miss Leota said firmly. "I presume you packed that large suitcase yourself, without anyone forcing you to fill it? Very well, it is your responsibility, not your brother's. If you want to take it now, I will carry your canvas bag. If you wish to leave it, do so. But please make up your mind. I do not wish to stand here debating the matter in the street all afternoon."

Benjy watched cheerfully as Fran handed her grandmother the carryall. Miss Leota took it and set off at a brisk pace down the sidewalk. Lugging his suitcase, Benjy followed her. Behind him, Fran staggered awkwardly under the weight of her own suitcase.

"Just you wait," she hissed to Benjy. "I'll get you for this."

☆ 3 ☆

A VOICE IN THE NIGHT

As Miss Leota had said, it was only a short walk to her house. They walked back up Congress Street, past the Lee-Jackson building Benjy had noticed on the way in, crossed the narrow intersection the bus had driven through, and walked a few blocks farther until they came to a neat red-brick church on their left. By that time, even Benjy's light suitcase was feeling heavy. He kept awkwardly shifting it from one hand to the other, and tried to concentrate on their surroundings instead of on his own tiredness.

Beside the church Benjy saw a white post with a hole in it. There was a funny sort of bomb or something lodged in the hole, and a tiny cannon perched on the top of the post, but he hesitated to stop Miss Leota to ask what it was. Then his interest was caught by a cemetery behind the church with some old, darkened tombstones. Miss Leota hurried them past the church and two more houses, and finally stopped at hers.

Benjy liked the house at once. There was a neatly trimmed lawn in front of the two-story brick house, and a small flower garden bright with new blossoms. A row of squared-off bushes lined the front walk, leading up to an impressive entrance with decorative white columns that stood out boldly against the red brick. The columns framed a spotless white door with a curved brass knocker hanging neatly in the center. When Benjy looked up, he could see that every window had a window box filled with bright flowers.

Miss Leota led her grandchildren to a side door off the driveway. "The front door and the parlor are really just for visitors," she explained, "and you two are family, aren't you?"

Benjy suspected that she hadn't yet made up her mind about claiming them as relatives. Maybe the front door was only for people she approved of. Somehow, using the side door made him feel like something less than a real person even if the front door *was* only meant for company.

Fran pushed Benjy aside, staggered into the little room beyond the side door, and dropped her bag. Without even looking at the attractive little chairs and tables set around to welcome friends, she tossed her hair back and leaned against the doorframe in an artificial pose of exhaustion. Her theatrics gave Benjy a chance to slip inside quietly and dump his suitcase and backpack. He flexed his sore muscles.

"That weighed a ton!" Fran gasped.

"Perhaps next time you travel, you will be more careful to pack only what you need," Miss Leota said mildly. She started down a hallway that led out of the little room. "Just leave those bags by the door. You can get them later when you go up to your rooms. Come along now, and I'll get you a snack."

Benjy followed her promptly, before Fran could pay him back as she'd promised for the disagreement over the suitcase. Miss Leota led him into a large, sunny kitchen with a high ceiling.

"Can I help?" Benjy asked shyly.

Miss Leota smiled at him and handed him plates and napkins to set out while she got some milk and opened a package of cookies.

"Thank you, Benjamin," she said. "I expect you're hungry after your trip."

Benjy nodded slightly. His grandmother sounded so formal. He couldn't tell if she wanted him there or not. Did she want to get rid of him and his sister, the way his mother had?

By the time Fran caught up to them, Benjy had set out the glasses of milk and was watching his grandmother put a cake with chocolate icing on the table.

"Did you bake that?" Benjy asked, feeling wistful. Their mother never did any baking anymore. She never even cooked anything special for them. She just said she was too tired from a hard day at work, and fixed something fast so she could fall asleep in front of the television set early.

Miss Leota looked at the cake with interest. "No, I'm sorry to say I didn't. Somehow I've gotten out of the habit of baking. Perhaps having you two around will inspire me once again."

"What do you do, Miss Leota?" Fran asked politely. She helped herself to a slice of cake.

"You might say I teach children," Miss Leota said.

"You're a teacher?" Benjy asked, surprised. Despite her energy walking home from the bus stop, his grandmother struck him as too old to cope with a classroom of kids every day.

"No," Miss Leota said. "I used to teach, but the school board decided to retire me. It's a foolish criterion, age—don't you think? Just because a person has lived for a certain number of years is no justification for assuming she is too old to be capable. Or too young, either."

Benjy nodded emphatically. He was beginning to like his grandmother. Even though she seemed stiff and formal, the things she said made sense. He wished his mother could hear Miss Leota—maybe then she'd quit telling him he was too old to be bugging her all the time for attention. And maybe the bigger kids in his class would stop telling him he was too young to hang out with them. Benjy started eating his piece of cake, carefully scraping the extra icing off the plate.

"I certainly didn't believe I was too old," Miss Leota went on, "but I couldn't convince the school board of that, so I was forced to retire."

"But you said you teach," Fran objected.

"I do," Miss Leota told her. "Now I write books that teach children the same things I used to teach them in my classroom."

"Books?" Fran asked, too surprised to hide her distaste.

"What sort of books?" Benjy asked, more interested in his grandmother than ever.

"History books," Miss Leota said. "Books about Southern history in particular, but some about English history as well. It's appalling how little children know about history these days."

"Southern history books," Fran muttered, shaking her head. She pushed her chair back from the table. "Thanks for the snack, Miss Leota. Can I go unpack now?"

"If you wish," said Miss Leota. "Keep going down the hall past the dining room, then go upstairs. Your room is the third on the right. Benjamin, yours is the first on the left. The bathroom you will share is at the head of the stairs."

"Thank you, Miss Leota," Benjy said shyly. He wanted to ask if maybe he could look at one of her books, but thought maybe he ought to wait until she offered. He didn't want to upset her, and have her make up her mind to dislike him like everybody else did.

Benjy couldn't make out what Miss Leota thought of him at all. She was being too formal to let any feelings show. At the same time, Benjy realized he hadn't let her know how much he wanted to like her. He didn't know how to start making friends. He wished he could find the words to reach out to her. It occurred to him that maybe she couldn't find the words either, that maybe all her polite conversation was just a cover because she didn't know how to start being a grandmother any more than he knew how to start being a grandson.

Wondering how they could make a start, Benjy headed out to the little room by the side door where they'd left their suitcases. When he saw Fran bend down to pick up her heavy suitcase, he offered, "Want me to carry that upstairs for you?"

Fran turned on him scornfully. "It's a little late for that."

Benjy shrugged, swung his backpack onto one shoulder, and then grabbed his own suitcase. The whole thing flopped open, sending the contents cascading all over the floor with a crash.

Benjy looked up from the clutter in time to see Fran hiding a grin as Miss Leota hurried into the room, demanding "What was that?"

"Just Benjy making a mess," Fran said cheerfully.

"He dropped his suitcase and spilled everything. Honestly, Benjy!"

"You opened the clasp!" yelled Benjy.

"Me?" Fran screeched, trying to look insulted.

"Benjamin," Miss Leota said sharply. "Did you see your sister tamper with your case?"

"No," Benjy stammered, "but I know it was closed before, and she stayed here when we went to the kitchen—she was laughing until you came in!"

"Why would I want to mess with your stupid suitcase?" Fran asked, sounding bored.

"Frances, I believe you wanted to unpack," Miss Leota said abruptly. "Benjamin, I suggest you collect your belongings and take them upstairs."

"But she—" Benjy spluttered, his face red.

"If you cannot prove that someone has done something," Miss Leota interrupted, "it is best not to try."

Benjy bent over his suitcase, trying to shove everything back in. He was furious with Fran. She'd made a fool of him in front of their grandmother, just for spite! He hated her. He wished he could take that monster suitcase of hers and swing it round and round and then smash her with it! If only he could get as far away from her as possible, and never see her again as long as he lived.

Clutching his bulging suitcase with both arms, Benjy fled down the hallway. So much for making friends with his grandmother! She'd never like him now.

"Supper will be at seven," Miss Leota called after them. "Please freshen up, and then come down early so you can help me get things ready."

Benjy rushed blindly up the stairs and veered left into the bedroom Miss Leota had said was his. He threw his suitcase and backpack into one corner and flung himself on the bed, trying to shut out the whole world. Too miserable to look at his new room, he lay facedown on the soft quilt until he heard Fran's footsteps start downstairs. Then he followed her slowly, wishing he could stay by himself. Sullenly, he helped set the dining room table. He could dimly hear Fran babbling on about an embroidered linen tablecloth and silver ornaments and real crystal glasses, but Benjy didn't even see any of them. He had made his mind blank, and didn't care.

Numbly, he heard Miss Leota say something about trying to welcome her grandchildren with a proper Southern meal—country ham and mashed potatoes, applesauce put up by a neighbor, sugar-snap peas, fresh rolls with damson plum preserves. Fran's voice buzzed around him about how delicious everything was. Benjy made himself eat what Miss Leota served him, but the wonderful food all looked gray on his plate and even the sweet preserves tasted dusty in his mouth. As soon as he could get away from the table, Benjy found his way upstairs again.

Safely behind his closed bedroom door, Benjy sighed

deeply. It was dark outside now, but he didn't want to turn on a lamp. He felt safer, somehow, alone in the dim light. Slowly the blankness receded, and he noticed soft moonlight coming through the windows. One of them was open, and on the cool evening breeze Benjy heard a distant singing.

> *Farewell, to the scenes of my childhood,*
> *To my mother, who's praying for me!*
> *She would weep if the son of her bosom*
> *From the face of a foeman should flee.*

Soft as the singing was, Benjy could make out each word distinctly. He felt his way through the shadowy room and looked out through the window. To his surprise, he found himself staring at the old cemetery he had seen that afternoon. The moonlight picked out the silhouettes of the tombstones, but Benjy could see no one standing nearby singing.

> *Farewell, to the home, to the hearthstone,*
> *Where my sisters are weeping for me;*
> *O the foot of the spoiler shall never*
> *Stain the home of the brave and the free.*

Benjy couldn't imagine his mother or sister ever weeping for him. He tried to laugh at the idea, but he couldn't manage even a smile. The clear tenor voice had an uncanny quality that sent chills crawling up his spine. He wished he could see the singer.

> *Ho for Liberty! Freedom or death, boys,*
> *That's the watchword—away let us go*
> *To the sound of the drum and the bugle,*
> *March to vanquish the ruffian foe.*
>
> *Adieu, honor'd father! who taught me*
> *For the rights of a freeman to stand—*
> *To resist, when his rod, the aggressor*
> *Shakes in wrath o'er my dear native land!*

Benjy shivered uncontrollably in the evening air. It was probably just some neighbor singing on his back porch, Benjy told himself, but he didn't want to hear any more. He backed away from the window in the eerie darkness and tripped over the mess from his suitcase. Fumbling frantically through his things, Benjy found his pajamas and struggled out of his clothes. With the singer's voice still echoing in his ears, he dived into bed, pulled the quilt up over his head, and tried not to think about the cemetery outside his open window.

☆ 4 ☆

LOCAL HISTORY

When the warm spring sun woke him the next morning, Benjy lay in bed feeling unusually peaceful. He stretched comfortably and took his first good look at the room around him. He lay in a deep, soft, four-poster bed piled high with extra pillows and covered with a quilt stitched in a swirling design of apple greens and sky blues. The same colors on a cream background patterned the wallpaper. Benjy liked the effect. It made him feel as though he were in the middle of a sunny field on a bright spring day.

He had been given a corner room with windows on two walls. Through one of them he could see another brick house across a stretch of lawn. The other, he remembered, faced the backyard and the cemetery. On the wall with the door Benjy noted a walnut bookcase, gleaming with polish. A small armchair upholstered in pale green nestled in the corner between the two windows. Then Benjy saw a large oaken chest of drawers and guiltily looked down at the mess from his suitcase. He jumped out of bed onto a soft carpet and hurried to unpack.

Once his room was neat, Benjy headed into the bathroom to clean himself up, too. To his delight, he found a large bathtub resting on four huge feet. Taking a bath was almost fun, imagining those immense feet belonging to some wild lion, racing through a tangled jungle. Back in his room he pulled on his faded jeans and a clean shirt and skipped downstairs. Without thinking, Benjy started humming the song he had heard the night before.

"Good morning."

Miss Leota's voice startled him. He stopped at the foot of the sweeping staircase and smiled at her uncertainly. Perhaps after last night she wouldn't want anything to do with him.

All she said, however, was, "You're up early," as she came into the front hall to meet him.

Benjy nodded. He remembered what he'd been thinking before Fran had tricked him. If Miss Leota hadn't already made up her mind to dislike him, maybe he could find a way to be friends with her after all.

"I like your house," he said awkwardly, "especially my room."

"I'm glad," she told him. "What was that tune you were humming when I interrupted you?"

"Oh." Benjy shrugged. "It's just a song I heard last night."

"Last night?" Miss Leota looked at him curiously.

Benjy nodded. She seemed interested, so he tried to explain. "Some guy was singing. I could hear him through my bedroom window, the one you left open. It was a strange sort of song—something about saying good-bye to mother and father and sisters and marching off with drums and bugles. I never heard it before."

Miss Leota had a faraway look in her eyes. " 'The Soldier's Farewell,' " she said softly. "I thought I recognized it."

"What is it?" Benjy asked, curious.

Miss Leota sighed. "A song from the War Between the States." She looked at him thoughtfully. "You say you heard it last night?"

Benjy nodded. "I looked out the back window, but I couldn't see anyone, just the cemetery." He shuddered a little. "Did you hear it too?" he asked hopefully.

"No," Miss Leota said. "I didn't. Well. Would you like some breakfast?"

Benjy felt starved. He nodded eagerly. "Can I help?"

"Certainly."

While they set things up in the kitchen for bacon and eggs, Benjy gathered his courage.

"Miss Leota," he finally began, "I was wondering—could I maybe see some of the books you've written?"

She stopped for a moment and looked at him. "Are you interested in history, Benjamin?"

Benjy nodded. "I like learning things," he explained shyly. He loved to read, even though it had been the reason for the teachers' putting him ahead a year in school. Reading books wasn't the same as having friends or being part of a real family, but it was some consolation. At least he could bury himself in a book and forget his problems for a while.

"Well, if you like history, you'll enjoy your stay here," Miss Leota said briskly. "Have you heard of the Battle of New Market?"

Benjy shook his head. "I saw a lot of things in town that seem to be named Battlefield Restaurant or battlefield whatever, or after General Lee or General Jackson, but I never heard of a battle called New Market before. Was it in the Civil War? Does it have something to do with that funny post I saw with the cannon on top when we passed by the church yesterday?"

Miss Leota nodded. "Whatever do they teach them in those Yankee schools?" she murmured. "Your teachers may have taught you to call it the Civil War, but that is not the correct name. It is the War Between the States. And Robert E. Lee and Stonewall Jackson were very famous Virginians who commanded armies on the Southern side during the War. One of the battles in the War was fought right through this town in 1864."

"Right here?" Benjy marveled. He forgot about feeling wary of Miss Leota.

"Each army held the town for a portion of the battle," Miss Leota explained as they sat down to eat. "That post was where the Confederate commander, General

Breckinridge, was almost shot down by a Yankee shell. The main clash occurred just north of the town."

"Wow." Benjy wondered about the battle as he ate his way through a hearty breakfast. "Who won?"

"We did, of course," Miss Leota said indignantly. "The South always fought well in the Valley."

"Tell me about the battle," Benjy begged.

"No," Miss Leota said, "I think you should go to the battlefield and learn about it firsthand."

"Is it still there?" Benjy asked, surprised.

"Oh yes," Miss Leota told him. "In the South we preserve our memories, and New Market was certainly a shining moment in our history. Go have a look today. When you get back, I'll loan you some of my books. One of them is about New Market," she added.

"Really?" Benjy grinned with anticipation, and Miss Leota smiled back. Then both he and his grandmother heard footsteps upstairs at the same time, and their smiles faded.

"I'd say that Frances is up," Miss Leota observed dryly.

Benjy ducked his head and bolted the last of his breakfast. Part of him wanted to stay and tell Fran about the battlefield and persuade her to come explore it with him, but a deeper part of him knew she'd never come, or if she did, it would be only to make fun of it. Benjy's excitement when his grandmother had told him about the battlefield had been so bright, he didn't want Fran to spoil it for him.

"I think I'll go see the battlefield this morning, Miss Leota," he said. "Then I could start reading your book about it this evening. Would that be okay?"

"That would be fine," she said. "Are you leaving now?"

Benjy looked up shyly and saw her staring evenly at him. Her blue eyes seemed to look deeply into him, and Benjy got the impression she saw very clearly how things stood between him and the rest of the world.

"Yes, ma'am," he said quietly. He carried his plate to the sink.

"The main battle was fought on the other side of the interstate," Miss Leota told him. "But you can see part of the battlefield and one of the monuments if you just go a few blocks farther up this street. Be alert for cars, though—this is also Route 11, and the traffic moves at high speeds. On the far side of the interstate there's a tourist center and a small museum in the larger part of the battlefield. Be careful crossing, and pay attention to the lights at the underpass you came in on yesterday. They'll give you a map and some pamphlets at the tourist center."

Benjy nodded. He ran upstairs for his jacket, and managed to slip out of the house before Fran had a chance to corner him.

Even though it was the beginning of May, the morning air was crisp. Benjy snapped his jacket up clear to the top and set off at a brisk pace to stay warm. He began to whistle the song he had heard the night before. What had his grandmother called it? "The Soldier's Farewell." Benjy wondered why she hadn't heard it. She and Fran had still been awake. Perhaps Fran had been chattering and Miss Leota couldn't hear over the racket.

He decided to go up to the monument Miss Leota had mentioned first. He passed some houses under construction and a retirement home, and then came to the Battlefield Motel. Benjy grinned. It sure was funny how everything around here seemed to be named after the battle. Back home in New York nobody he knew made this kind of fuss about history. Past the motel was a rolling, rocky field, and Benjy decided that must be the battlefield.

He ran up closer and saw some signs and a map of the battle action posted beside the road. He was on the far right side of the Confederate line, he figured out from the map. Apparently the most exciting part of the battle had taken place over by the cluster of buildings he had seen from the bus the day before.

A white board sign hung on the fence that surrounded the field. DO NOT ENTER was painted on it in big red letters. Benjy hated to run clear back into town, cross under the interstate, and then go all the way back up to the battlefield when he was so close now. Maybe he could find some shortcut across the field. Suddenly feeling unusually daring, Benjy decided to climb over the fence. That was the sort of thing the other kids at school bragged about doing all the time, but Benjy was always too sure he'd make a mess of things to ever try following them. He'd do it wrong—and then everybody would laugh at him worse than ever. But who was to know here in New Market? Even if he failed, no one would ever hear about it. And if he got over the fence, he could climb to the high ground a little farther on. From there he'd be able to see the rest of the battlefield and the interstate, and find some better way across.

Benjy took a quick look around. No cars were coming, and nobody seemed to be watching him. He carefully set one foot halfway up the woven wire fence just beside a fence post and tested it. The wire sagged a little, but it held his weight. Benjy gripped the post with both hands, gingerly lifted himself up, and swung his right foot over the strand of barbed wire on the top and hooked it into the other side. He freed his left foot, and vaulted awkwardly into the field.

Immensely proud of himself, Benjy jumped up and ran to the higher ground. He was in luck! At the far side of the field, he could see a square concrete culvert cutting right through the foundation of the interstate. And just above it, beyond the roaring traffic, were the tops of the buildings on the battlefield.

Benjy set off at a run. The field was rocky and uneven, though, and he slowed to a walk after tripping a few times. He was already out of breath—he wasn't used to this much exercise. At home, he hardly ever ran around outdoors. It was too boring to play alone when he could sit inside with a book.

The culvert was tall enough for him to walk through easily. A trickle of water ran down the center of the floor, but the rest of it was dry. Under the interstate, Benjy could hear the traffic's noise reverberating all around him. He hurried through and found himself just a little downhill from the stone and board houses. As he ran eagerly toward them and saw the trees nearby, he suddenly remembered the strange sight he had witnessed from the bus. This was where he had seen that solitary tree shaking so crazily!

Benjy looked around. Which tree had it been? They all looked the same up close. He was half afraid if he got too close to it, the tree might throw some sort of fit and attack him. Or had an unseen somebody actually been shaking the tree? Benjy had looked hard, but perhaps the person had been hiding.

Nervously excited, Benjy walked up to the nearest tree and gave it a shove. It stood firmly, its leaves barely trembling. Benjy tried harder to jiggle it, but still got no response. He ran to the next tree and tried again, beating at it with all his might, but nothing budged. How could the tree have waved so wildly the day before? Why couldn't he make any of them move today?

Benjy staggered to another tree and hammered at it

with his fists. The rough bark scraped his hands, but he couldn't give up. He had seen the tree shake! Why couldn't he make it happen again? Sometimes it seemed to Benjy that everybody else in the world was always making things happen, but he constantly smashed head on into everything he tried. His breath came now in great, uneven gasps, and he almost reeled into another tree. A few leaves fluttered down around him, but the tree remained steady. Benjy shut his eyes and fought back the tears.

"What do you think you're doing, Mister?"

Benjy jumped at the unexpected question. He had been certain no one was watching him! Slowly he turned to face his antagonist, his sore fists already clenched.

Standing to one side of the tree was a boy only a little taller than Benjy. His fists were resting on his hips, and he was studying Benjy with a perplexed expression on his face. But it was the boy's strange outfit that surprised Benjy even more than the fact that he had snuck up on him.

It was some sort of military uniform—a funny pair of baggy gray trousers stuffed into a pair of dark leggings that buttoned up the sides, and a gray tunic buttoned up to the neck. Perched on the boy's dark hair was a strange gray cap with a wide, flat bill. The uniform looked like a soldier's, but Benjy couldn't imagine the army taking anyone so young. He wondered if the boy was some sort of security guard and was going to throw him out of the battlefield.

The boy straightened up and fixed Benjy with a strange, aristocratic expression. "Well, sir, what were you doing?" the boy repeated. There was something curiously familiar about the voice.

Suddenly Benjy knew who the boy was. He sputtered, "It was you singing last night!"

☆ 5 ☆

THE CONFEDERATE SOLDIER

The boy's gray eyes narrowed abruptly. "What singing?" he demanded warily.

Now Benjy was certain. The clear tenor voice was sending chills up his back just as it had the night before.

"'The Soldier's Farewell,'" Benjy stammered. "I heard you singing from my window, but when I looked, I couldn't see anybody."

The boy smiled. It was a fleeting, otherworldly smile that gave Benjy a funny, shivery sensation.

"Why were you hiding?" he blustered, hoping the other boy wouldn't realize he was scared.

"I was not hiding," the boy snapped. "And you have not said why you are running about beating upon these trees."

Benjy blushed. He couldn't expect anyone to believe his story about the tree shaking by itself yesterday, but that was his only excuse. And Benjy didn't want this boy to think he was crazy; he wanted the boy to like him. If only he could find the right words to explain about the shaking tree!

"Yesterday," he began cautiously, "I was riding in a bus along that road up there." He pointed to the interstate. "When we passed this field, I saw one of these trees shaking, but the others were all still. And there wasn't any wind," he added, "not even a breeze."

The boy pushed his cap farther back on his head and peered at the interstate. "You saw someone shaking the tree?" he asked. Benjy thought his casual tone sounded forced.

"That was the funny part," Benjy said slowly, keeping an eye on the boy. "I couldn't see anybody near the tree."

The boy nodded, sighing. Benjy felt sure it was a sigh of relief.

"It was you, wasn't it?" he said. "You were hiding both times!"

"I hide from no one, sir!" the boy insisted, his eyes snapping angrily.

"Well, maybe I just couldn't see you in the dark last night," Benjy conceded, eager to prevent the boy from getting angry at him, "and you did come up quietly today. But there was lots of light yesterday afternoon, and I was watching real carefully, and I know I saw the tree shaking all over the place but I didn't see you anywhere!"

"I was looking for something," the boy admitted grudgingly. "But what business is it of yours? And who are you? I have never seen you here."

"I'm visiting my grandmother in New Market," Benjy explained. "I just came over to explore the battlefield. Why are you asking me all this? Do you work here or something? Is that why you're wearing that uniform?"

"I do not work here, I belong here," the boy said, clearly insulted. He tugged at his tunic and straightened his cap and held his head at an arrogant angle. "I am a Cadet at the Virginia Military Institute. This is the uniform of a Cadet!"

"Oh." Benjy was impressed. Then he felt confused. "How can you belong here, then? Isn't the Institute an hour away at Lexington? And what were you looking for yesterday? Maybe I can help you find it."

Suddenly, from the orchard past the cluster of houses, the two boys heard voices. Benjy turned and saw several people who were studying a map and some pamphlets walking across the battlefield. He turned back to ask the boy again about his peculiar behavior—but the strange Cadet had disappeared!

Benjy looked around frantically. He couldn't see the boy anywhere. How could he have vanished so quickly? Benjy had only turned away for a second. He frowned. Why had the boy given him such an eerie feeling? And he'd gotten away without even explaining what he was looking for, or how shaking the tree was supposed to help him find it. Another thought struck Benjy—if this boy was a Cadet at the Virginia Military Institute, what was he doing out in the middle of the night singing songs in a cemetery?

Maybe he's on spring vacation too, Benjy told himself. Maybe he's staying with friends or relatives in town. At any rate, the boy was gone now. Benjy shrugged and started walking toward the large, round building with the flags flying. He figured that had to be the tourist center. Suddenly he felt a sharp stab of frustration—he hadn't even found out the boy's name!

Disgusted with himself, Benjy trudged up to the information center. A polite lady gave him a map and a pamphlet, and offered him a small booklet about the battle for seventy-five cents. Benjy decided to buy it and went over to a small, deserted seating area so he could start reading them.

As near as Benjy could make out, a Northern general named Franz Sigel had marched into the valley in 1864, planning to cut across the mountains at a pass called New Market Gap. Looking at the map, Benjy could see why New Market was so important—the Gap just southeast of the town was the only way across those mountains.

On the other side of the mountains, General Robert E. Lee was commanding several armies containing most of the Confederate troops in Virginia. These armies, Benjy read, were trying to stand off overwhelming numbers of Yankee soldiers on a series of four different battlefields between Washington and Richmond. If General Sigel succeeded in crossing New Market Gap, the Northern Army would come out behind General Lee and could crush the main Confederate Army between two enemy forces. So the last available Confederate soldiers had mustered under a General Breckinridge to march up to New Market and stop the Yankees. Even the Cadets from the Virginia Military Institute were called out! Benjy was surprised to read that some of the Cadets had been just fifteen years old. They were only a little older than he was. Benjy shivered, imagining himself marching off to battle.

General Breckinridge had intended to hold the VMI Cadets in reserve, deeply concerned that the possible loss of young lives would threaten the future existence of the Confederacy. As the Southern line advanced against heavy fire, forcing the Yankees to withdraw, part of the Confederate Second Brigade fell back in disarray. A hole was left in the Confederate line. If the Yankees had charged into the hole, they could have split the Confederate line and turned the tide of battle!

Instead, the Cadets were ordered to fill the break in the line. Under a raging storm of musket balls and cannon fire, the boys marched forward in perfect order and filled the hole just before the Yankee charge. The Confederate line and the Cadets held firm, and when the Yankee charge was broken, the order to advance was given. The Cadets surged forward, in their enthusiasm outdistancing even the veterans on either side of them, and captured a battery of Northern cannons. The Yankees broke in wild retreat and ran from the field. The Battle of New Market was won!

Benjy sat back, sighing with satisfaction. He could hardly wait to go outside and find the place where the Cadets had marched up to fill the hole! They must have been awfully brave, with those musket balls and cannon shells flying all around them.

Across from the seat Benjy had chosen was a painting hanging on the wall. It seemed to be a picture of the VMI Cadets charging the Union artillery. On the ground were several bodies, and for the first time Benjy realized that some of the Cadets must have been killed in that terrible hail of gunfire.

One Cadet on the far right side of the painting had just been struck by a bullet. The force of the shot had thrown him back, and he was falling helplessly as his schoolmates marched past him. In his right hand he was still clutching a musket that looked taller than he was.

Staring at the Cadet, Benjy's stomach lurched in sudden shock. Although the dying boy's face was unfamiliar, he was wearing a neat gray uniform. Down to the funny dark leggings buttoned up the sides and the flat-billed gray cap that was flying off as the boy's head snapped back, it was a uniform that Benjy recognized all to clearly.

☆ **6** ☆

A FAMILIAR FACE

Maybe VMI Cadets still wore the same uniform?

Benjy tried to convince himself, but he had the sinking feeling that clothing had changed too much in the past hundred and thirty years for that to be true. Benjy saw again the eerie, otherworldly expression on the strange boy's face, and remembered how quickly he had disappeared—almost as though he had vanished into thin air. The boy had said he belonged at the battlefield. . . .

A dreadful fear lodged deep in Benjy's stomach. Could he have seen the ghost of one of those Cadets who died to stop the Union Army at New Market?

That would explain the unseen force shaking the tree and the disembodied voice singing the long-forgotten song outside his window. But why would a ghost have appeared to him?

Perhaps the whole thing had been an accident. Benjy considered the possibility. The boy had been awfully surprised that someone had seen him shaking the tree and heard him singing. Somehow, the two of them must have stumbled onto each other by chance.

Benjy frowned. That wasn't the way ghosts were supposed to behave—they haunted people because they wanted something. What could a ghost want from him?

Confused, Benjy sighed. If only he'd found out the boy's name. Maybe he could have found him on a roster or some sort of list of the VMI Cadets who were killed in the battle. But he'd let the boy get away, and he had no idea how to find him again.

Maybe Miss Leota's book would give him a clue! The more he could learn about the battle and the Cadets' participation in it, the better prepared he'd be if he ever saw the boy again. Benjy decided his exploration of the battlefield could wait. Clutching the map and booklet and pamphlet, and taking a last look at the picture of the dying Cadet on the wall, Benjy jumped up and hurried back to his grandmother's house.

"Miss Leota!" he cried, pulling open the side door. He ran panting down the hallway. His legs felt like lead—Benjy couldn't remember a day when he'd run around so much.

"Miss Leota!" he called again, skidding to a halt in front of the staircase.

"Good heavens, Benjamin!" Miss Leota hurried out into the front hall. "Whatever is the matter?"

Benjy shook his head, badly winded from his run.

"Nothing," he managed to gasp out. Suddenly he remembered that he was a guest in her house. Would she be angry at him for running in and acting as though he felt at home? He still wasn't sure whether or not she had accepted him as a member of the family.

"I'm sorry," he stammered. "I shouldn't have run in like that. But I wanted to see your book on the Battle of New Market. Could I, please?"

Miss Leota folded her arms across her chest and looked at her grandson thoughtfully. "Your apology is accepted. I take it you enjoyed your visit to the battlefield?"

Benjy nodded enthusiastically. "Could I look through your book? I want to find out more about the Cadets from VMI."

"Ah, yes." Miss Leota looked as though she suddenly understood his excitement. "I can see how you would be interested in the Corps of Cadets. I'll find that book for you; I believe I have a copy in my office."

Benjy finally caught his breath and began to calm down. While Miss Leota went into a room off the hallway, he remembered Fran. Glancing upstairs warily, Benjy wondered if she was waiting for him with some new torment. Maybe he should take the book back to the battlefield so he could read it undisturbed.

"Here you are, Benjamin," Miss Leota said, coming out of her office with a crisp copy of her book. "I'm sure I needn't tell you to take good care of it."

"No, ma'am." Benjy took the book eagerly. "Uh, Miss Leota—is Fran upstairs?" he asked.

"No," his grandmother reported coolly. "She went out earlier."

Benjy grinned. "Then I'll go up to my room to read. Thank you, Miss Leota."

She nodded and returned to her office. Benjy looked quickly at the picture of several Confederate soldiers on the book cover and started up the stairs two at a time. He was sure he could find some answers now!

The book was exciting reading. Benjy began to understand something about how the boys of VMI had felt when they joined General Breckinridge's army on its march to New Market. Many of them had fathers and brothers who had already been killed fighting the Yankees. A lot of them had families living on the land the Union army would march through if they reached the New Market Gap and crossed the mountains. Like in that song he'd heard the night before, the soldiers were passionately concerned with defending their homes and their families from the Union troops who planned to destroy them. And the boys at VMI had been so eager to fight! A few of the youngest Cadets even cried when they had to stay behind because of their age.

Benjy imagined the Cadets marching proudly up to New Market, eager to defeat the Yankees. They must have known that some of them would die in the battle—and yet they were eager to be a part of it. Benjy remembered reading that the Civil War, or (he corrected himself) the War Between the States, had begun because of a disagreement about slavery. He had never been able to understand how anybody, especially a boy his age, could care so deeply about an idea like slavery that he would be anxious to march off and die for it. Perhaps the books he'd read had oversimplified the causes of the war. Benjy could imagine how someone might care enough about his home and his family, and the threat of another army invading his country and telling him how to live his life, to be willing to risk death.

Benjy felt a twinge of bitterness. If he'd been alive then, would he have been willing to give up his life to protect his mother and sister and to make his father proud of him? Not likely! Benjy couldn't think of anybody he cared enough about to go to battle for. After all, nobody cared that much about him.

Benjy heard the phone ring but didn't pay much attention to it. He jumped in surprise when Miss Leota called him a few moments later.

"It's your mother," she announced as he ran down the stairs.

Benjy took the receiver in amazement. "Mom?"

"Benjy? Hi, honey—how was the bus trip? Did you get in okay?" Static crackled on the line, and his mother's voice sounded tinny and thin.

"I'm fine, Mom," he told her, watching Miss Leota

disappear down the hall into her office. "How about you?"

Her laughter tinkled in his ear. "Oh, Benjy, I feel wonderful! Not having to go to that office for a little while—it's as though a weight has fallen away. I feel free. Do you feel like that about being out of school?"

"I guess," Benjy said doubtfully. His mother sounded so young all of a sudden. He couldn't remember when she'd sounded so happy before.

"Only I miss you and Fran," she went on. "Are you two getting on all right? How do you like New Market?"

"We're okay," Benjy said. "New Market's great. I've been to the battlefield and it's really exciting."

"Good for you!" His mother hesitated a moment. "How are you getting on with your grandmother?"

Benjy wasn't sure how to answer that. Finally he said simply, "I like her—I like her a lot."

"That's wonderful." Mrs. Stark sounded relieved. "What about Fran? Your grandmother said she was out?"

"You know Fran," Benjy said. "She's just mad at not getting her own way."

His mother laughed again. "You're so wise for your years, Benjamin Stark! Oh, honey, I'm so glad I caught you in. You'll give Fran my love, won't you? And Andy's too?"

"Sure, Mom. Where are you, anyway?"

"Vermont—we're just going to drive around and stay at different motels. It's such a change from the city! I've already sent you each a postcard—you should be getting them any day now."

"Thanks." Benjy grinned in spite of himself. She knew he loved getting mail.

"Well, I've got to go now. I love you, honey."

"Bye, Mom."

Benjy hung up the phone, still grinning. He hadn't forgiven her for shipping him off the way she had, but he felt good about the call. And he felt great about the postcard.

He went back to his room and found his place in Miss Leota's book. He stretched out across his quilt and read about the Confederate and Union troops fighting back and forth for possession of the town of New Market. Benjy was so engrossed he didn't hear the side door slam or even realize Fran was back until she strode into his room.

"Got your nose buried in a book again?" she sneered. "Honestly, Benjy, don't you ever get an urge to get out and do anything? No wonder you're so boring!"

Benjy concentrated on his book. He'd already decided that Fran was the last person in the world he'd ever tell about his adventure at the battlefield that morning. She'd find the whole story hysterically funny, and she'd never let him forget it. He hoped she'd just go away.

"Well, I've been exploring New Market," she announced.

Benjy looked up. "Good for you," he said. "You missed Mom's call."

"She called?" Fran looked shocked. "You're kidding."

"She said to give you her love," Benjy said. "And Andy's."

Fran made a face. "So what?"

"She said she's in Vermont," Benjy went on. "She sent us postcards."

"Big deal," Fran said sullenly. Then she brightened. "I've been making friends. You know there are two colleges in Lexington? That's just over a hour away from here. One of them is a military school, and I met some of the Cadets who were visiting people in New Market—they are really cute."

Benjy wondered how he could ever have imagined their trip might bring them closer together again just because they were in a strange town. No matter where she was, Fran made friends quickly, especially boys. And with new friends to occupy her, she would forget all about Benjy.

"What about your plan to get out of here?" he reminded her. "Tantrums and all that?"

"You are really dumb." Fran gave him a superior smile. "I was just pulling your leg, Benjy. It's so easy to make you mad!"

Benjy stared hard at his book, refusing to look at Fran. He wished he could get back at her, but he got so frustrated whenever she started taunting him. He wanted to shout, "Get lost, go back to your great new friends! I don't need you!" but it wasn't worth the effort. He knew it wouldn't make any difference to her.

Fran didn't wait for him to say anything. "There's this one guy—he's a Cadet at VMI—his name's Robert." She smiled. "Some of us are going to drive down to Lexington tomorrow, so I'll see him again. He is so cool."

Benjy shut her out. Who cared about her great new friends? Benjy was going to make friends of his own, friends a lot better than hers. He was willing to bet Fran had never seen a ghost in her life, let alone talked to one. He ignored her when she waltzed out of his room.

As soon as the door shut, Benjy flipped through the rest of Miss Leota's book. There were lots of maps and pictures in it that got him right into the action. After one chapter he found several pages of pictures of Confederate soldiers. He recognized their neat gray uniforms right away, and looked closer. These were pictures of the VMI Cadets who had died in the battle! Frantically, Benjy scanned the pictures until a familiar face leaped out at him.

In the faded, old-fashioned portrait, the boy sat rigidly, staring fixedly at the camera. His unwieldy, man-sized hands were balanced awkwardly on skinny knees. But the dark hair and the aristocratic expression on his determined face were unmistakable. This was surely the boy Benjy had met at the New Market battlefield! But that boy must be dead. . . .

☆ 7 ☆

THE GOLD WATCH

"Cadet Private William Hugh McDowell," Benjy repeated to himself as he trotted across the field to his culvert the next morning. All his doubts about the boy being a ghost were forgotten—he could think only about the excitement of making friends with a ghost. He and Miss Leota were starting to become friends; couldn't he do the same thing with the Cadet he had done with her? How many other friends could a ghost have, after all?

When Benjy emerged on the other side of the culvert, he stopped and looked around. He was a little winded from the hike, but it had seemed easier than the day before. He wondered how to find the boy.

Benjy walked up to the nearest tree and gave it an experimental push. He looked around expectantly, but no one was there. He leaned against the tree and thought hard. The boy had said he was looking for something. Benjy didn't have the faintest idea what it was, but it occurred to him that maybe if he started looking also, the ghost would get scared he might find it first and come stop him.

On the other hand, someone else might come stop him first. On the map they'd given him the day before at the tourist center, there were rules against digging around in the battlefield or using metal detectors to look for war relics. Benjy didn't want to attract the wrong sort of attention.

So he tried just calling the ghost. "Hey, Cadet William Hugh McDowell! Remember me? I'm Benjy Stark, from yesterday!"

The named sounded awkward, so Benjy tried shortening it. "Cadet McDowell!" he shouted. "William McDowell, where are you?"

Exasperated, Benjy started chanting, "William McDowell, William McDowell, William McDowell—" Finally he ran out of breath, and his voice quit on him.

For a moment he just stood there, breathing hard but determined not to give up. Then, all of a sudden, he felt prickles tickling the back of his neck like they always did when someone was watching him. The last thing he needed was anyone sticking his nose into his discovery. Furious at being spied upon, Benjy spun around.

To his surprise, he found himself face to face with the strange boy from yesterday—Cadet William Hugh McDowell!

"You came!" Benjy cried, delighted.

"Of course. You gave me no choice, sir." The boy sounded irritated. "You are shouting my name all over the place as though you were a madman."

"I didn't know how else to find you," Benjy explained, suddenly worried he'd made the ghost angry. It was like walking a tightrope, this making friends! "I've been reading about the Battle of New Market—I know who you are now."

"So I see," Cadet McDowell remarked. He pushed back his cap and looked at Benjy with a troubled expression. "What is it you want of me, anyhow? I am no magic genie."

"I know, you're a ghost," Benjy said. "My name's Benjy—can I call you William?"

The Cadet sighed. "My friends called me Hugh."

"Why?" Benjy asked. No one he knew used their middle name.

"Hugh was my grandfather's name," the boy said. "What kind of a name is Benjy, anyway? It sounds like a small child's name—aren't you too old for that?"

Benjy drew himself up and tried to look older. At least Hugh was only a couple of inches taller than him, so he didn't have to feel too much of a shrimp. "I'm thirteen—almost," he declared.

Hugh nodded. "Your name is Benjamin? You should use Ben now, or even Benjamin if you'd prefer." He grimaced. "My mother called me Willie, and I detested it. But my grandfather always called me Hugh, and my father usually did. Once I arrived at VMI I made certain my friends used Hugh."

"I do sort of like Ben," Benjy said thoughtfully. It sounded more grown-up than Benjy, but still kind of friendly.

"Ben." Hugh bowed slightly. "Now then, what is it you want? Why did you summon me?"

"I just wanted you to come back," Benjy said uncertainly. "I mean—I thought maybe since I'd seen you shaking the tree and heard you singing and seen you yesterday and everything—I just thought we could be friends. After all, haven't you been haunting me?"

"Who is haunting whom?" Hugh asked wryly. "I have not invaded your home rattling chains or slamming doors, have I? You are the one who continues to come here and pry."

"I'm not prying!" Benjy said hotly. "If anyone's prying, it's you—what were you doing singing outside my window, anyway?"

"I knew nothing of the people living at that house." Hugh shook his head. "I came to the cemetery—I was buried there for three years after the battle. Then they moved our graves to the Virginia Military Institute." He looked out over the battlefield unhappily. "I stay here, but occasionally I return to the site of my old grave, just to rest. I was not trying to haunt you—I was just singing a song that gives me pleasure."

"You said you were looking for something," Benjy pressed. "Why were you shaking the tree out there where anybody could see it? Is something hidden in the tree? And what if you do find it, anyway? Don't you know there's rules against taking war relics from the battlefield?"

"Rules?" Hugh demanded. "This is my battlefield!"

"It was in 1864," Benjy pointed out, "but this is more than a hundred years later!"

"As I well know." Hugh slumped unhappily. "That, Ben, is my problem."

"What do you mean?"

"That is why I cannot find it," Hugh explained. "Everything is different."

Benjy sat down on the grass and looked at the dejected Cadet. "What can't you find?" he asked.

"My watch," Hugh said, sighing heavily.

"It was my grandfather's gold watch." Hugh settled down beside Benjy, leaning his elbows on his knees, and went on to explain that very few men of his own time actually owned watches because they were so expensive. Most people estimated the time from the position of the sun. But when his grandfather started in the tobacco trade, he had vowed to himself he would buy a gold watch as a symbol of his success. Hugh looked up, his eyes shining with pride in his grandfather.

"He was finally able to put together a huge crop of

tobacco leaves—he even traveled to England with the shipment, to make sure no one would cheat him anywhere along the way. Then he went to London with his profits, and bought a beautiful gold pocket watch and had it engraved with his name. It was very precious to him."

"How did you get it?" Benjy asked, impressed.

"He had always intended to leave it to my father after his death," Hugh went on, "but then he changed his mind. I was his eldest grandson, and I was his namesake, so before I left for VMI he had the watch engraved with my name and the year my class would graduate, 1867. He believed in me, I know he did! I think he wanted to show me that I could become a man once I got away from home. He gave the watch to me the morning I left for school, and it meant everything to me."

"How did you lose it?" Benjy asked gently.

"I am shamed by my stupidity!" Hugh groaned. "The excitement must have addled my reason. I always wore the watch because it was so special to me—I could reach down and touch it, and it was as though my family were right beside me. I could see my grandfather standing there, looking so proud of me. . . . The watch made me feel worthwhile, just knowing it had been a part of my family and now it was a part of me."

Hugh shook his head. "I was on guard duty the night General Breckinridge's orders arrived, so I was wearing the watch then. After that, we were all so rushed and excited as we packed our kit and set out upon our march that I never even recalled it until we were half-way to New Market!

"Actually," Hugh admitted, "I felt glad in a way, once I realized I was still wearing it. Even though we were eager to whip those Yankees, we were still a little nervous underneath. At least, I was. Having that watch with me helped me remember my father and my grandfather and our home, and what the War was all about. I just wish I'd left well enough alone."

"What do you mean?" Benjy asked. "What did you do?"

"I took it off," Hugh told him.

"You what?" Benjy cried. "Why?"

"You cannot imagine how terrible that battle was, Ben," Hugh tried to explain. "All around me soldiers were falling shot, and many of them were dying. The battle seemed to be going both ways at once. The Yankees had us outnumbered, and they knew they had to get through that mountain pass just as we knew we had to stop them! When those soldiers ahead of us began to retreat, I had a dreadful vision of what would happen if the Yankees surged forward and won the field."

Hugh was shaking his head, his gray eyes dark, bottomless pools at the memory. "They were scavengers, Ben. They'd rifle the pockets of a dead Confederate—

they'd steal a dead man's wedding ring if they thought they could get something for it later! No Confederate would let them cross those mountains, so if the Yankees won it meant all of us would be dead, and I knew I couldn't risk some damn Yankee taking my grandfather's watch for a souvenir!"

"So what did you do?" Benjy whispered.

"I hid it," Hugh said simply. "When I was shot, I took it off and hid it where the Yankees would never find it! Only, I had no way to tell any of my people how to come get it, either."

"So it's still here," Benjy said, looking around the battlefield with wondering eyes. "Well, it's safe, isn't it? The Yankees didn't get it."

"But my family never got it either," Hugh said bitterly. "They thought I'd lost it. I'm sure my father never felt I deserved the watch to begin with, no matter what Grandfather thought. If I leave it here forever, just turn my back on it as though it were a trifle of no consequence, I would be turning my back on all the generations of my family. I would be turning my back on being a McDowell. I cannot do that, Ben. I cannot rest in peace until I recover my family's watch."

Benjy swallowed. Had any member of the Stark family ever felt such a responsibility to their family honor? He couldn't imagine it. He couldn't imagine himself taking something like a watch so seriously. But he could see how important it was to Hugh. This wasn't just a story out of the past—for Hugh, this was still happening. And if Benjy wanted to try to be friends with the Cadet, it would be happening to him too.

That was a frightening thought. Benjy had never gone out of his way to do anything important for anybody else before. No one had ever bothered to get involved in his life, either. Was that what being friends meant, being willing to get involved to help a friend when he needed it? Part of Benjy wanted to run away from the battlefield and the responsibility of helping Hugh. He'd wanted a friendly ghost to have fun with, not a problem to solve. And he didn't notice Hugh asking him about his problems and offering to help shoulder the load. But if each of them waited for the other to reach out first, would they ever become friends? Hugh needed a friend now, and Benjy made up his mind to try.

"So," he said slowly, "the watch is here, but you can't remember where you hid it."

"I remember," Hugh insisted, "only nothing looks the same as it did then!" He gestured impatiently at the interstate with its traffic roaring past them. "Men came and cut that monstrosity straight through the battlefield and shoved earth up all over the place—now the ground itself is a different level than it was then! And the buildings are a travesty! The buildings we fought our way through began to collapse as the years passed. Then strangers came along and carried away the rotten wood and altered the foundations and built their own version of the old farm buildings on top!'

"But where did you hide your watch?" Benjy asked impatiently.

"In a crack in the rocks!" Hugh snapped.

"Which rocks?" Benjy demanded in exasperation. There were rocks everywhere, after all, buried deep in the valley soil. Had Hugh tried to bury his watch under a rock somewhere and now the ground was all messed up?

"I'm not exactly certain," Hugh finally admitted.

"But you said—"

"I know what I said!" Hugh interrupted. "But I had been shot—I could hardly see and I knew I was dying, and I just cannot recall clearly what happened. I only remember crawling through the mud. My mind was filled with the watch. It was a sacred trust which I had to protect from the scavengers. Suddenly I saw this space between two rocks, all dark and shadowy. I pulled my watch out and wrapped it up in the oily rag from my musket, and stuffed it into that space. It fit so perfectly—as though the crack were made for it. Then I lay back and stared at the sky and felt the rain on my face—and that's all I remember."

Benjy looked around the battlefield. "You were headed toward those buildings and the orchard beyond, weren't you?"

Hugh looked over at the restored farm buildings and

nodded. "My company was marching directly toward the main house, just beside that shop building."

"It has a stone foundation," Ben said eagerly. "Could you have gotten that far forward and found a crack between the stones and slipped your watch in there?"

"But it doesn't look the same!" Hugh cried. "There are no cracks—hardly any of the foundation is left at all!"

"You said the ground is higher because of the interstate," Benjy pointed out. "The crack could be below ground level now!"

Hugh looked up, his gray eyes glowing. "You really think so, Ben?" he asked softly.

"It's worth a try," Benjy said, feeling an excitement growing inside himself that he could hardly recognize.

"Then we shall do it!" Hugh jumped up and whooped enthusiastically.

"Hold on a minute," Benjy cautioned. "They'll stop me if they see me digging around here—they have rules about that, too. How about if we wait until after dark? I think I can get in through that culvert at night—then no one will notice us!"

"Tonight, then," Hugh said. "When will you come?"

Benjy figured in his head when his grandmother ought to be asleep and he could tiptoe down the stairs safely. "Around eleven-thirty or midnight?" he suggested.

"I'll be waiting for you," Hugh promised.

"Hugh," Benjy started curiously.

"What?" the ghost prompted.

Benjy got to his feet and brushed off his jeans. "Well, after all these years—I mean, wouldn't the battlefield have been easier to look through if you'd tried sooner? Why didn't you recover your watch right after the battle, when the place still looked pretty much the same to you?"

Hugh shrugged and looked down at the ground between them. "I could not have moved it anyway," he finally said. "A ghost cannot handle a real object. I did look, though. My hope was that if I could learn where it was, then perhaps I could find someone to take it out for me."

Benjy stared at the Cadet. "No one else has ever seen you before, have they?"

Hugh shook his head, not looking up. "Not once in nearly one hundred and thirty years. There must be something special about you, Ben." He raised his eyes and stared intently at the living boy. "Perhaps you truly can help me recover the watch and do what is needed."

"What do you need?" Even through his rising joy over Hugh's calling him special, Benjy could tell just how important this was to the Cadet.

Without hesitation Hugh said, "My family must know I kept our honor. They must know I did my duty."

"Okay," Benjy agreed. "After we find the watch, you need me to take it to your family. Where are they now?"

Hugh shook his head. "I don't know, Ben."

"Well, how do you expect me to give it to them?" Benjy demanded, exasperated.

Hugh looked at him. "They'll know at VMI," he said. "They care about remembering us there. They'll know how to find my family." His eyes fell. "At least, I pray they will, Ben. It is my only hope."

"Don't worry, we'll find your watch, Hugh," Benjy tried to assure the ghost. "And I'll get it to VMI safely, too. That much I promise!"

☆ 8 ☆

LOCKED IN

Benjy walked into the front hall to find a full-scale fight in progress.

"Why can't I go?" Fran was shouting at their grand-mother. "This is supposed to be my vacation, you know! All I want to do is get out with my friends and have some fun!"

"Don't raise your voice in my house, Frances," Miss Leota said evenly. "You may not drive down to Lexington this afternoon if you intend to stay there all evening, and that is final."

"But why?" Fran shrieked, flinging her hair behind her. "You have no right—"

"I have every right since you are in my care," Miss Leota informed her. "First of all, you said you would not be back until after midnight. That is much too late for a sixteen-year-old girl to be out. And secondly, these friends of yours, as you call them, are seventeen- and eighteen-year-olds. You are too young for their activities."

"That's a laugh!" Fran snarled. "I'll be seventeen this summer, and all my friends at home are seventeen or older. Mom lets me go out with them whenever I want!"

"Unfortunately your mother is not here to give you permission," Miss Leota began, but Fran hurried on.

"And there's this really cool guy who likes me—what's Robert going to think when I don't show up?"

"If he is a young gentleman as well as a 'cool guy,' he will think you have a family who values you too much to let you run around unsupervised until all hours," Miss Leota said mildly.

"A 'young gentleman'?" Fran laughed wildly. "What is this? Did I get off that bus and take a step backward about a hundred years?"

"Perhaps," Miss Leota said agreeably.

"You don't tell Benjy what he can do and not do!" Fran yelled, catching sight of her brother.

"That is because Benjamin has shown himself to be extraordinarily responsible and comes and goes as he should," Miss Leota said with a sigh.

Benjy felt his face burning. If Miss Leota had any idea what he and Hugh had planned for tonight, she wouldn't think he was so responsible! He began to worry. With Fran causing all this fuss, how was he going to slip out to meet Hugh?

"Well, I'm going with them and you can't stop me!" Fran snapped, starting up the stairs.

"I shall lock the doors," Miss Leota said pleasantly. "Without the house keys, you will be unable to open them. Unless you wish to leap from your window to join your friends, you will remain here."

Fran's only response was to run sobbing to her room and slam the door.

Miss Leota winced as the house shook at the impact. Then she sighed and smiled at Benjy. "Did you have a good day, Benjamin?"

Benjy nodded. Inside he felt blind panic. How was he going to meet Hugh if the house was all locked up tight? At home, no one ever cared when he or Fran came in or left. It felt strangely reassuring that Miss Leota did care, but it was an inconvenient night for it.

Fortunately, Miss Leota didn't feel like talking. She looked weary after her clash with Fran. "There's a post-card for you on the hall table, Benjamin," she said quietly. Then she walked slowly to her office.

Benjy grabbed his postcard and ran up the stairs two at a time. Inside his room he tried to think what to do. Could he jump out of one of his windows? Miss Leota's suggestion had been sarcastic, but he might be able to climb down even though Fran wouldn't dare.

He checked each window. On one side it was a straight drop down, and he suspected he'd make a terrible racket landing even if he managed not to break a leg. But below the other window, the one facing the cemetery, a sloping roof jutted out from the house and protected a little paved area with wrought-iron chairs and a curved concrete bench. If Benjy could creep down that roof without making too much noise, maybe he could jump onto the bench from the roof's edge. Whether or not he could climb back up the same way he had no idea, but he felt better having a plan of escape.

He remembered his postcard and looked at it. There was a picture of thick green trees with a little brook running between them. It looked cool and peaceful.

"Dear Benjy," his mother had written. "Isn't this beautiful? It's a world away from offices and the city and work and worry. I hope you're enjoying your vacation as much as I am. We all need a break in our routine sometimes. Thank you for understanding. Andy sends you his love. We'll see you soon!"

Benjy looked at the trees for a while. He still didn't like the way his mother had sent him here, but he had to admit he was enjoying his vacation. He propped the postcard up on his dresser and picked up Miss Leota's book.

Supper started out to be a grim affair, with Fran sitting there red-eyed and sullen. She certainly wasn't enjoying the break in her routine one bit. Benjy decided to ask Miss Leota about the behavior of Northern soldiers during the War between the States. It shouldn't tip Fran off to his ghost, but it would give him a chance to learn whether Hugh had been right to worry about his watch. He might have just been paranoid.

"Miss Leota," he ventured, "during the War, did the Union soldiers really strip bodies and steal from the dead Confederates?"

His grandmother looked up from her plate with an astonished expression. "You mean the Yankees? Whatever have your schools taught you, Benjamin? When the Yankees invaded our land, they burned farms and fields, they slaughtered our livestock, they murdered innocent men and women, and they stole everything they could. Many Southern families buried their valuables to try to prevent the Yankees from finding them."

"You mean money and things?" Benjy asked.

"More than money," Miss Leota told him. "They tried to preserve their family heirlooms. They would bury such things as silver plate, or treasured jewelry, or a silver tea service, or a clock. Money could be earned from the land, Benjamin, but an heirloom that had been handed down from one generation to another, perhaps even traveled with a family member from their old home in Europe to the New World, could never be replaced. To a Southern family, such a legacy was far more valuable than money, for these objects represented honor, and a reverence for their family heritage. It was unbearable to think that such treasures might be stolen." Miss Leota's voice sounded bitter. "To the Yankee 'souvenir hunters,' a family's precious heirlooms were worth nothing more than the money they would bring."

Benjy frowned. "That doesn't sound like the way soldiers ought to act. Didn't they get into trouble?"

"Their officers were as bad as the men," Miss Leota said tartly. "What has your mind been filled with? I suppose you haven't read any Southern histories of the War, but. . .haven't you even seen *Gone With the Wind*?"

Benjy made a face. "Yeech. All that kissing and stuff!"

Miss Leota laughed. "There's a good deal more to that story than some silly twit of a girl and her romances! Seriously, Benjamin, you could learn a lot about our love of our land and our hatred of the Yankees from that film. Nearly every Southern family lost some precious heirlooms to a Yankee scavenger."

Benjy nodded. So Hugh had been right to be afraid. It seemed hard to imagine people acting like that, but maybe during a war right and wrong got turned inside out and people did whatever they could get away with. But that didn't excuse stealing.

"Honestly," Fran hissed at her brother when Miss Leota went to the kitchen for the dessert. "Buttering her up like that! You never cared about the Civil War before!"

"I never knew enough about it before," Benjy retorted. "Now that I'm here, it's pretty exciting."

"I'll bet," Fran sneered. "You're just sucking up to Miss Leota. Well, don't bother—she won't like you any more than anyone else does. Nobody ever likes you!"

Fran was wrong for once, Benjy realized. He'd always believed the mean things she'd said about him before, and that's what made them hurt so much. But he knew better this time. He wondered if she hadn't always been right before. Maybe he'd been too willing to accept what she'd said, to help put himself down. Maybe he should stand up for himself more.

Benjy wished he could tell her about Hugh. Hugh liked him, Benjy was sure of it. And Miss Leota had even come right out and said she approved of him. "I've already made a friend here, over at the battlefield," he told his sister, "and he likes me, so there!"

"Oh, sure," Fran said. "What is it this time, some imaginary friend? You are so weird, Benjy."

"He's no more imaginary than your cool Robert," Benjy said hotly. "Hugh's real!"

Miss Leota returned before Fran could answer him. Benjy sat there, smoldering. How could he convince Fran his friend was real? How do you make someone believe in a ghost?

After supper, Fran stormed upstairs and shut herself in her room again. Benjy decided to try to get to sleep early so he'd be ready for the search, but lying under his quilt with the lights out, he felt wide awake. He couldn't stop asking himself why he was doing this. He didn't know how he was going to climb down the roof, much less how he and Hugh were going to find the watch in the dark. Why was he even going to try?

At home, Benjy never would have done anything

like this. He couldn't even climb a chain-link fence at school without tearing his jeans or getting cut, or even play ball at lunchtime with the other kids without fumbling the ball and looking stupid. And yet he'd come up with the idea to go treasure hunting in the dark with Hugh, and every day now he'd been climbing a wire fence to cross a field to sneak through a culvert, and now he was going to risk falling out of a window to run around in the middle of the night with a ghost! All because Hugh needed his help.

No one had ever needed Benjy or had ever believed in him—not his overworked mother or his carefree father or any of the bored teachers at school or his malicious classmates. Until Hugh. And Hugh believed Benjy was the one to help him. Because Hugh needed him, Benjy would do whatever he had to do. Hugh was his friend.

Benjy woke with a start. He wasn't sure when he'd fallen asleep or what time it was now. He grabbed for his watch and checked the illuminated dial—it was eleven o'clock. Benjy slid out of bed and tiptoed across the floor to his door. He listened first, then peeked out carefully. No lights were on in the house, and the other bedrooms were silent. Benjy pushed his door shut again and hurriedly dressed, trying not to think about the climb down the roof. He picked up a flashlight and his battered pocket knife.

Benjy hefted the rusty knife sadly. He'd been so proud when Mike had given it to him. Mike had dated his mother for several months, and he'd always found time to talk to Benjy. Sometimes he'd even play ball with him, or talk to him about things the other boys already knew. He'd gotten Benjy the knife, and promised to go camping with him sometime and teach him how to build a campfire and take care of his knife and everything, and Benjy had been really excited. But then Mike had stopped coming around, and when Benjy asked his mother when Mike was going to take him camping, she'd told him Mike was gone for good. The knife had gotten rusty and dull, and Benjy didn't know how to sharpen it or make it shiny again.

Sighing, he hooked the flashlight onto his belt and slid the pocket knife into his jeans pocket. He could read all the books there were, and his teachers could keep on promoting him ahead of the other kids and filling his head with book facts—but a book couldn't teach him how to be a man. That was something a father was supposed to do. Benjy had been hoping that Mike could teach him, but Mike didn't stay around any more than his father had. Still, Benjy kept the pocket knife with him. It was better than nothing.

The sloping roof looked much more dangerous in the dim, patchy moonlight than it had earlier. Benjy edged the window up as quietly as he could, sat on the windowsill, and swung his legs out. Carefully he eased his legs down until he was holding the windowsill with his fingers and lying on his stomach on the roof.

His sneakers were braced against the roof's shingles.

Slowly, Benjy took one hand off the sill and gripped a lower shingle instead. Then he took a deep breath, told himself very firmly not to be afraid, and let go of the sill with his other hand.

There was a bad moment when his free hand couldn't seem to find a shingle, but Benjy made himself stay calm, and finally his damp palm slid down one row of shingles and he hooked his fingers over the next one and held tight. After that, inching his way down row by row didn't seem so terrible.

His sneaker scraped a loose shingle once, and he was afraid everyone had heard. For a second he clung to the roof, waiting for the lights to flash on, but the unexpected noise must have sounded loud only in his own ears, because the house remained dark and silent.

One foot finally brushed the gutter, and Benjy knew he had to look down. He steadied his grip and turned his head, and breathed a sigh of relief. He was positioned directly over the concrete bench. Carefully he lowered himself until he was hanging from the edge of the roof by both hands. His feet dangled just above the bench.

Why couldn't he have been a few inches taller? Benjy cursed his height silently. Even just a couple of inches would have meant his toes might have been able to feel the bench beneath him. But wishing wouldn't make him grow. Benjy looked down one last time and asked himself whether this was really necessary. Flexing his arms, knees, and body, he ordered himself to relax, took a deep breath, and let go.

Benjy almost couldn't believe it. He landed lightly on the bench with a soft thump. He hadn't missed it, he hadn't slipped and fallen off, he hadn't done anything wrong! He, Benjamin Stark, had climbed down a roof in the dark and survived—not only survived, succeeded!

Feeling like a conquering hero, Benjy jumped off the bench and slipped out of the backyard. Now to find Hugh!

☆ 9 ☆

THE SEARCH

Even in the shadowy moonlight the old cemetery failed to look sinister. Hugh had said he had been buried there for three years, Benjy remembered. Knowing that made the place seem somehow more friendly. Benjy raised one hand in salute, then ran past the leaning, almost overgrown tombstones to the sidewalk and up the road to his usual fence crossing. He scrambled up the woven wire footholds, vaulted over the strand of barbed wire, and hurried across the field.

In the dark, Benjy's familiar culvert took on the appearance of a gloomy, threatening cavern. He paused at the entrance and tried to see into the blackness, but he could make nothing out. When he crossed in daylight, Benjy could always see the battlefield with its wooden buildings and white rail fences waiting on the far side. With its pathway dissolving into darkness, the culvert seemed to have no end.

Benjy took a deep breath and reminded himself that

Hugh was waiting on the other side. He ducked his head and made a mad dash through the murky culvert, the thumps of his sneakers echoing hollowly off the surrounding concrete tunnel. Then he was back in dim moonlight on the other side, gasping for breath and looking wildly around for his friend.

"You came!"

Hugh's voice took Benjy by surprise. He spun around to find the ghost grinning at him.

"Keep your voice down," Benjy started to warn him, but then he realized no one else could hear Hugh anyway, so it really didn't matter.

"Sorry I took so long to get here," Benjy whispered. "I had to sneak out after everyone was asleep—I climbed down the roof and everything," he announced proudly.

"Well done," Hugh told him. "Shall we look first at the wheelwright shop?" He pointed to the restored shop building they had chosen earlier.

"What's a wheelwright shop?" Benjy asked curiously.

"They make wooden wagon wheels there," Hugh explained. He examined the shop building doubtfully. "Do you truly believe digging around the foundation will work?"

"If the ground level has been raised since you hid the watch there," Benjy said confidently, "then it's just a matter of digging down and checking the gaps in the stones underneath." He studied his ghostly friend curiously, remembering that Hugh had said a ghost couldn't handle something real. "I guess I'll have to do the digging, but you can do the checking. Your eyes are probably better in the dark, anyway."

When they reached the shop building, Benjy knelt on the damp earth and prodded the ground gently. He tried scooping some of the dirt out with his fingers, but it was studded with loose rocks and packed in pretty hard. He dug into his jeans and pulled out his old pocket knife. Even though the ancient blades were rusty and dull, he could use it to loosen up the dirt so he could get it out.

"Wherever did you get that thing?" Hugh demanded when he saw the knife's battered condition. "Has no one ever taught you how to care for your knife?"

Benjy shook his head. "No," he admitted unhappily. Now Hugh wouldn't like him either. No one ever liked him once they found out he couldn't do anything right. They just made fun of him. If Hugh laughed at him—Benjy waited to feel the rising anger that other kids always provoked, but it wouldn't come. He realized he was hoping, desperately, that the ghost wouldn't laugh. Benjy had never made the mistake of thinking of the other kids as friends, but he wanted to be friends with Hugh—he had reached out to the Cadet. If Hugh was really his friend, he couldn't laugh.

Instead, Hugh sighed in amazement. "You need a whetstone to sharpen it, for a start," he explained, "and you ought to oil it lightly so you can move the blades smoothly. Always wipe it off before you put it away, and that will keep the blades from rusting. Do you understand?"

Benjy nodded, wordless in his relief. Hugh hadn't laughed—instead he'd tried to teach him what to do. It hadn't sounded hard—Benjy was sure he could do the things Hugh said. He felt pleased at the thought, and started to dig eagerly at the packed dirt.

"Hurry up," the ghost said impatiently. He hovered over Benjy as though his presence would speed the younger boy along.

"I'm trying!" Benjy told him, breathing heavily from his efforts. "This ground is hard, you know!"

"Perhaps a shovel would work better," Hugh suggested, backing off slightly.

"I didn't have room to pack one in my suitcase," Benjy retorted rudely. He was still jabbing at the rocky dirt with his knife.

"Don't be angry," Hugh said. "I was only trying to help. You and I are in this together now. It is a pity we cannot get inside this shop. Look at all these tools."

Benjy looked up to see Hugh standing on the other side of the white rail fence, looking inside the open wall that displayed the interior of the shop building to tourists. He jumped up to join him. "But I can't get past those bars. If only you could slip inside and push something out to me!"

"Unfortunately it doesn't work that way," Hugh said ruefully. "Being a ghost is not all people think it is. But what about those things over there?"

Benjy looked around. Hugh was pointing toward the main farmhouse. In the yard beside the house, Benjy could just make out some vague shapes silhouetted against the white boards of the house. Squinting through the patchy moonlight, he tried to focus more clearly on them, but the clouds scudding across the sky kept him from seeing anything distinctly. "What is it?" he asked.

"Let's have a closer look."

Hugh led the way down the path with Benjy at his heels. Carefully checking the deserted battlefield to make certain no one could see him, Benjy pulled his flashlight off his belt and directed its dim beam at the shadows beside the house. In the soft light he could see a sawhorse sinking into the muddy dirt. Beside it, a couple of tools were propped up.

"I see a broom and a saw," Hugh said, "but no shovel. Too bad there isn't a hoe or something like that. Who could have left these things?"

"Somebody working on maintenance or repairs must have left them there after work," Benjy said. "Good luck for us that they did."

He left the path to investigate. There were a few more tools lying on the ground. "Look!" he cried, holding up one of them. It looked something like a pick.

One tip of the blade ended in a sharp point, but the other widened slightly and curved out into a flat scoop. "This ought to do! It's pretty heavy, but I can dig with this flat end!"

Hugh looked closer. "It's a mattock, Ben—it will do. Now try again."

Benjy made his way back to the path, then looked behind him. His sneakers had left huge footprints in the mud. "Oh no," he said. "What are we going to do about those? Someone's going to know we've been here!"

"Don't worry," Hugh told him. "First of all, whoever left those tools out will not tell anyone for fear of making trouble for himself. And we can cover your tracks with leaves or something afterward."

Benjy nodded. There wasn't much he could do about it now anyway, even if Hugh was wrong, so he hurried back to the place he had started digging before.

Awkwardly swinging the heavy mattock, Benjy scraped the ground ineffectually.

"Have you never used a mattock before?" Hugh demanded.

Benjy sighed. He couldn't seem to do anything right. "No," he admitted.

"Oh." Hugh watched for a minute longer, then said, "Look, Ben, let me show you how to handle it. You lift it up in the air with both hands," he explained, demonstrating with his own arms upraised over his head. "Then you swing that flat blade straight down until it sticks in the ground. Pull up on the handle until the surface of the sod breaks, and then pull the dirt back toward you."

Benjy lifted the mattock and tried to follow Hugh's directions. The Cadet nodded in approval. "Much better, Ben!"

Benjy grinned, delighted with his unexpected success. He could learn to do things right, if someone would only take the time to help him. Then Benjy remembered figuring out how to climb over the fence and cross through the culvert to reach the battlefield, and how to climb out of his bedroom window after Miss Leota had locked the doors. If he stopped to think, he could make himself find a way to succeed. He'd just never tried before.

Eagerly, Benjy attacked the hard earth. Soon he had opened a narrow trough several inches deep along the front side of the foundation. He threw the heavy mattock aside and lay down on his stomach to peer into the space.

"Have you found it yet?" he asked Hugh hopefully. But the ghost kicked at the loose pile of dirt Benjy had thrown up and shook his head.

"Nothing," Hugh muttered. "Look for yourself—there are no spaces between those rocks anywhere!"

Benjy switched on his flashlight again and quickly scanned the foundation stonework. Hugh was right;

the stones seemed solidly packed. Benjy sighed and snapped off the light.

"Could you have gone around one of the sides?" he suggested. "I can try digging there."

Hugh shrugged. "I don't think so. It's no use, Ben! The foundation looks the same all around."

"It's worth trying," Benjy insisted. Despite his aching shoulders, he grabbed the awkward mattock again. Along the side facing the barn there was a small wooden shed, and Benjy extended his trough partway around it. But just as Hugh had said, all he uncovered was the same solid-packed stone foundation. Where could the crack between the rocks be?

Benjy rested a moment and stared at the buildings around them. He shivered slightly in the chilly gusts of wind. The clouds seemed to be thickening overhead, but Benjy didn't want to worry about getting rained on. He had to figure out what had happened to Hugh's watch. There was one other building on this side of the main house that might have been the one Hugh had crawled toward. Could they have chosen the wrong shop building to begin with?

"Hey, Hugh," he called softly. "What about the blacksmith shop, over there—could you have gone to it?"

Hugh glanced at the second shop building, way to the right of the main house. He sighed. "Perhaps—but it's very far from where we were. My Company was aiming just left of the house. How could I have gotten way over there?"

"Well," Benjy decided, "it's worth a try. We can't seem to find anything here."

Ignoring the damp gusts of wind, Benjy ran to the blacksmith shop dragging his mattock and started digging. Even though he carved out a trough along both the back side facing the Cadets' advance and the side nearer to the position of Hugh's Company, all he uncovered was the same solid stonework they had seen at the first building.

"Nothing," he groaned. Frustrated at himself and at the coming storm and at the impenetrable stone foundations, he hurled the mattock across the grass. It bounced heavily and struck a tree, then fell to the ground.

"What was that for?" Hugh asked. He sounded surprised.

"I tried, I really did," Benjy said, his voice shaking. He dropped onto the wet grass, so furious at himself that he could barely keep from crying. "I had to climb down the roof and I had to run through that awful culvert and I've dug and dug and I just don't know what else I can try! What am I supposed to do?"

"Nothing," Hugh said simply. He came and dropped down on the cool grass beside Benjy. "You did try, Ben, I know you did. There's nothing else you can do."

"But what about your watch?" Benjy demanded,

shocked. He sat up straight, his self-pity set aside. This was no time to throw a baby's tantrum.

Hugh shrugged. "I'll continue to search. I have faith I will find it someday."

"But what happens when you do find it?" Benjy cried. "Who'll take it to VMI for you? Who'll find your family?"

"I'll manage," Hugh told him distantly, putting an end to the topic. It sounded as though he was putting an end to their friendship as well. "Ben, you should put that mattock back in the yard and go on home to bed. There's nothing more we can do."

But Benjy couldn't bear the thought of giving up yet. He didn't know what more he could try, but he did know he couldn't just walk away from the battlefield and give up on his growing friendship with Hugh. He couldn't give up on himself this time. Hugh had said earlier that they were in this together, and he was right. Both Hugh's honor and Benjy's future depended on their recovering the watch. Benjy knew he had to succeed.

He turned away from the ghost and started slowly pushing the loose earth back into the trough he had dug around the blacksmith shop. "Maybe we can't get any farther digging up the foundations of these buildings," he said while he worked, "but there has to be something else we can try—something entirely different."

"What?" Hugh asked. Benjy could tell from his tone that the ghost didn't believe him at all.

"I don't know." Benjy shoved the last of the dirt back into the ground and stood up to tramp it down firmly.

"But I do know one thing, Hugh." Benjy turned to stare down at the ghost, lying prone in the grass. "I know I'm not just going to go back to bed and give up. I've promised to help get your watch back and I'm going to do it! I don't know for sure just how yet, but I'll figure out some way. We're going to find that watch, and I'm going to take it to VMI for you and try to find your family and that's all there is to it!"

With that, Benjy spun away from the astonished Cadet and strode over to the mattock. He picked it up, carefully checked it for any loose blades of grass and wiped it on his jeans to make sure it was clean. Then he replaced it exactly where he had found it in the yard. He was trying to sweep some dead leaves over his footprints in the mud when Hugh came up behind him.

"I apologize, Ben," he said quietly. "I never expected you would care enough to want to keep trying. No matter how important it is to me, what difference could it make to you? I thought you would give up and want to get back to other things that are more important to you."

"You're my friend," Benjy said, and was surprised at

the way his voice broke suddenly. He swallowed. "What could be more important than that?"

"I thank you, Ben," Hugh said softly.

Benjy shrugged off the thanks awkwardly, then he grinned.

"Allow me to take care of these tracks," Hugh offered. He leaned over and blew the leaves. The air swirled as though a cold breeze had taken the place of the storm winds whistling through the yard, and the leaves scuttled about in the draft, settling over the telltale footprints.

While Hugh was blowing the leaves into place, Benjy went around to the far side of the wheelwright shop and started packing the loose dirt back into the first trough he had dug. He couldn't understand why there were no cracks whatsoever in the stone foundation. Hugh had remembered seeing them—how could they have disappeared since then?

He was almost finished when Hugh rejoined him with the news that the yard looked normal again.

"What do you think we should try next?" the ghost asked.

Benjy pushed the last of the dirt into place and sat back in the damp grass, yawning. "I don't know," he said slowly. "My mind isn't working just now. Let's get together tomorrow morning after I've gotten some sleep, and see what we can come up with then."

"A fine plan," Hugh said, nodding. "How much time

do we have, anyway? When does your visit with your grandmother end?"

"Not for a few more days," Benjy told him. "I don't leave until the seventeenth."

"Really?" Hugh sounded pleased. "Then you'll be here for the battle."

"Come on, Hugh," Benjy muttered, half asleep. "That was over a hundred years ago."

"Time for bed," Hugh said suddenly. "You're nearly asleep on your feet. Shall I walk you home?"

Benjy nodded sleepily. He had long ago stopped worrying about how he was going to climb back into his bedroom, but he hated the thought of venturing into the black, echoing culvert all by himself again. With Hugh beside him, it didn't seem so threatening.

The two boys crossed the rocky field together. The clouds were so thick Benjy could barely see his feet. Several times he stumbled on the uneven ground, but he made it to the fence and succeeded in pulling himself over. By the time they reached Miss Leota's house, Benjy was ready to be tucked into bed.

"Where did you climb down?" Hugh asked.

Benjy pointed toward the backyard and led Hugh around to the little covered patio. "I went down the roof there, and then dropped onto that concrete bench." He shook his head sadly. "I don't know how I'm going to climb back up, though. I'm too short to reach the roof, even from the bench."

Hugh looked at him steadily. He was only a few inches taller than Benjy. "When you're always too short for things, you must devise ways to compensate," he said firmly. Benjy guessed his friend had had lots of experience compensating for his height.

Hugh was looking around the paved area. "There," he said suddenly. "That should give you a couple extra inches." He pointed to some pieces of wood stacked neatly by the back door, and Benjy remembered seeing a fireplace in the living room. The wood must have been left over from the cold weather.

"But won't somebody notice the wood on the bench tomorrow?" Benjy asked. It didn't really worry him, though; he had already started to the woodpile to pick up a few thick pieces. He was so tired all he wanted was to crawl under the covers and get to sleep.

"Don't worry," Hugh reassured him. "After you're in bed, I can blow the wood down. They will suppose that some dog ran past and knocked the woodpile over, or that the storm blew it down."

Benjy nodded sleepily. "That's a good idea."

With the extra height the wood gave him, Benjy was able to get a good grip on the edge of the roof. He was wondering how he could find the strength to heave himself up when he heard Hugh's voice.

"Come on, Ben—you can do it."

Benjy told himself if Hugh thought he could, then he must be able to do it. So he held on tightly to the roof, flexed his knees, and pushed himself off from the pieces of wood. At the same time, he heaved his body up with his arms, and suddenly he was stretched out on the sloping roof, one sneaker hooked onto the shingles at the roof's end and his hands still clutching the edge. He pulled the other foot up and braced himself more securely, then called softly down to Hugh, "I did it!"

"I knew you could," Hugh told him matter-of-factly. "Now get on up to bed."

Benjy got himself turned around and discovered it was much easier to crawl up the roof than it had been to inch down it. He could see where he was going, for one thing, and knowing that Hugh was with him gave him greater confidence. In no time he reached his bedroom window and vaulted over the sill into his room.

Leaning back out, Benjy waved to Hugh. "See you tomorrow," he called softly.

Hugh nodded. "Good night," he called.

Benjy stripped off his clothes, pulled on his pajamas, and slipped under the covers. Then he heard a soft thumping clatter as the pieces of wood tumbled to the ground. He smiled, pleased with Hugh's idea. Only then did he recall what Hugh had said at the battlefield. The memory of the ghost's words sent a chill feeling creeping up from the small of his back and jarred him wide awake again.

Then you'll be here for the battle. . . .

☆ 10 ☆

FAMILY PORTRAITS

Benjy woke the next morning to the sound of rain beating against his windows. He started to sit up in bed and groaned at his sore muscles. He ached in places he'd never even felt before! Stiffly, he eased his tender body upright and stared at the storm.

Overnight the winds had increased, and the rain was driving hard against his windows. To his dismay, Benjy discovered he had left the window partly open after his return last night, and he now had a puddle under it. Worse still, he'd dropped his clothes on the floor, and they lay under the opened window, soaking wet.

Irritated at himself for not thinking, Benjy jumped out of bed, winced at his sore legs, and bent down to check his jeans, shirt, and jacket. After a moment, he decided it had been more a stroke of luck than a disaster. After his digging through the muddy battlefield last night, his clothes were pretty filthy. This would be a good excuse to wash them without having to explain to his grandmother how he'd gotten them so dirty.

Benjy took a quick bath in his friendly tub with the big feet and pulled on some clean clothes. He shut the window and used a couple of his bath towels to mop up the floor underneath. Then he hurried down to tell Miss Leota.

"Good morning," she greeted him cheerfully. "I see the storm did not disturb your sleep?"

Benjy glanced at the grandfather clock in the hallway. It was after nine! What with all the excitement last night, he really had overslept. But he shook his head in answer to her.

"No, I slept fine, Miss Leota," he said, "only I had a little problem."

"A problem?" she asked. "What sort of problem?"

Benjy grinned sheepishly. It was sort of funny, after all. His mother would have yelled at him, but he didn't think Miss Leota would be angry. "I slept so well I never heard the storm start, so I didn't get up to close my window. The way the wind's been blowing, a lot of rain blew in."

Miss Leota sighed. "Oh, dear."

"It's not too bad," Benjy said quickly. "You see, I sort of dumped my clothes on the floor last night, and they were under the window, so they soaked up most of the rain. And I mopped up the rest with my towels, so there's not any mess to speak of. Really."

Miss Leota chuckled. "I suppose you have discovered the one situation in which untidiness can be a blessing," she told him. "Are you sure there's not any more mess for me to clean up?"

"None at all," Benjy assured her. "Only, do you have a washer? My jeans and stuff were kind of dirty anyway, and since they're all wet now, it'd be a good time to wash them. I could throw the towels in, too."

This time Miss Leota laughed. "You certainly have a way of seeing the bright side of all problems, Benjamin. Well, bring the things downstairs and I'll wash them for you."

"Oh, that's all right," Benjy said quickly. "I know how to do laundry—I do mine at home a lot."

"You do?" Miss Leota asked. Benjy couldn't quite make out her expression, but he didn't think she approved. But if his mother was too tired after work and he ran out of clean clothes to wear, somebody had to wash them, didn't they?

"Very well," Miss Leota said, sighing. "The washing machine and dryer are downstairs, through the doorway on the left side of the kitchen. The detergent is in the cupboard above. Call for help if you have any questions."

"Thank you, Miss Leota," Benjy said appreciatively. He ran upstairs, hoping his grandmother wouldn't notice his stiffness as he favored the worst of his sore muscles, and grabbed the bundle of his dirty clothes and the damp towels. Then he dumped it on the floor and pulled out some dirty socks and underwear as well.

If he was going to do some washing, he might as well get everything clean at once.

"All in?" Miss Leota asked him after he had left the machine sloshing.

"Yes, ma'am," Benjy said.

"Then how would you like some breakfast?"

"Great," Benjy said eagerly. "I'm starved!"

He helped her set out the breakfast dishes and made the toast while she fixed him eggs and bacon. "You sure do make good breakfasts," he said as they sat down at the table together.

"Thank you," Miss Leota said. "I believe a good breakfast is the most important way to get each day off to a good start."

"Where's Fran?" he asked suddenly, remembering her outburst last night. He hadn't heard her this morning at all.

"She's out," Miss Leota said briefly.

"Out, in that?" Benjy asked, amazed. Fran hated going out in the rain. She said it messed up her hair and clothes.

"Frances insisted on going out this morning to find her friends," Miss Leota explained. "After forbidding her to go last night, I felt I could not say anything today.

"But what about you, Benjamin?" she asked, leaving the subject of Fran. "You always seem to be off by yourself. Have you made any friends here yet?"

Hugh! Benjy choked on a piece of bacon as he remembered he was supposed to meet Hugh today to work out a plan. But how could he get there in this storm? Benjy decided that Hugh would understand. Maybe that's why Fran had gone out in the storm, because she was afraid her friends would drop her if they had the chance.

"Are you all right?" Miss Leota demanded, concerned.

Benjy coughed and tried to nod. "I just breathed at the wrong time, Miss Leota," he managed to gasp. "I'm sorry."

"That's quite all right," she said, "as long as you're sure you're all right."

"I'm fine," he said, a little hoarsely. "Friends? I guess I just don't make many friends," he told her. Sitting across the breakfast table from Miss Leota, listening to the drumming of the rain against the windows, Benjy felt at home. He relaxed and admitted to her, "I can't do any of the things they do, like playing ball and stuff. So I just read a lot, and sometimes I go off on my own. But it's okay. I'm having a great time here, I really am."

"Yes, I had gotten that impression," Miss Leota said slowly. "Perhaps you'll tell me about your adventures someday."

Benjy nodded, concentrating on the last of his eggs. He didn't want to accidentally mention anything about being with Hugh last night. And he didn't know whether he could tell his grandmother about Hugh at all, if it came to that. Maybe she'd understand about a ghost, but if she didn't, then she wouldn't like her grandson anymore—she'd think he was a liar, and she wouldn't want any more to do with him. If their friendship was going to succeed, that was a risk he couldn't take.

"Well, what are you going to do today?" Miss Leota asked, tactfully changing the subject. "I don't think it's the best day for going to the battlefield again."

Benjy shook his head. "I've almost finished your book about the battle," he told her. "Could I maybe borrow another of your books?"

"Certainly," she said, pleased. "Reading is an excellent way to spend a rainy day. And I must admit I am delighted you enjoy my books."

"They're great," Benjy said. "They're not at all like the Civil War history books at school—I mean, the War Between the States. Anyway, your books are really interesting."

"I'm glad they're interesting," Miss Leota said, "but I can't be too pleased you've been taught so little Southern history. You come from a long line of Southerners, Benjamin, and you should have been taught more of your heritage."

Benjy squirmed in his chair. "I can't help what they teach in school, Miss Leota."

"Of course you can't," she said quickly. "I simply

wish your parents—" She interrupted herself and sighed. "It doesn't matter. After all, you're learning now. Do you know about Stonewall Jackson?"

Benjy thought for a minute. "He was a famous Confederate general," he said slowly, trying to remember what he had read. "I've seen all kinds of things named for him around town, here. He got his men to rally around him by standing like a stone wall, something like that, right?"

"Exactly," Miss Leota answered. "In 1861 and 1862 he was the great defender of the Shenandoah Valley. He marched his troops up and down the Valley between the Yankee armies, using the Massanutten Mountain as a shield. He confounded the Yankees at every turn."

"Wow." Benjy was impressed. Then a thought occurred to him. "If he was so good at protecting the Valley, why didn't he chase the Yankees out of New Market?"

Miss Leota sighed. "He was dead by then, unfortunately. However, he was a great man while he lived. I've written a book about him, also. Perhaps you would like to try that one today?"

"Sure," Benjy said eagerly.

While she tidied up the kitchen, Benjy trotted downstairs to put his clean things into the dryer. Bending down to load the dryer made his sore shoulders ache again, but he tried to ignore them. The soreness would go away in time, and anyway, helping Hugh was worth it. He was relieved to see that all of the mud had vanished from the clothes he had worn the night before. Only a few faded grass stains remained, but Benjy wasn't worried about those.

By the time he came back up from the basement, Miss Leota had disappeared. He wandered back toward the front hall, figuring she had gone into her office to find that book for him, and met her coming out.

"Here you are, Benjamin," she said, handing him a book with a picture of a stern man with glowing, almost hypnotic eyes on the cover. "I hope you enjoy it."

"Thanks," Benjy said happily. "I'm sure I will."

"If you need anything," she told him, "I'll be in my office."

"I'll be okay," he assured her, and watched as she went back inside her office and closed the door.

Even with the new book, Benjy felt restless. He was angry at the weather. He should be at the battlefield with Hugh, making plans! They only had a few more days before he and Fran had to leave for home—there wasn't any time to waste. But with this storm he was trapped indoors for the day.

Restlessly, he walked up and down the hallway, wishing he could make the rain stop. But he couldn't even shut out the sound of it, beating against the house. In the front hallway, past the grandfather clock, he caught sight of the front parlor. Even though they'd been at Miss Leota's for several days, he had only glimpsed the room through the doorway in passing. Curious, Benjy decided to explore.

It was shadowy in the overcast morning. Benjy got the impression the room was full of intricate furniture and knickknacks. The walls were hung with paintings. Beside him, a tall lamp with a fringed shade threw a long shadow stretching from the hallway deep into the room. Behind him, Benjy could hear the grandfather clock ticking menacingly.

Abruptly, he reached up and pulled the chain on the lamp. It clicked on and a hazy golden light filled the room. Benjy gasped. The furniture was beautiful, the sort of chairs he'd be afraid to sit on for fear of breaking one. The seats were covered with hand-stitched needlepoint patterns, and the wood was lovingly polished to a warm sheen. On a corner table there was a collection of photographs in shining silver frames. Benjy went closer.

Although they were obviously old and some of the pictures were cloudy, he could make out a couple of shots of a young woman who looked a lot like Miss Leota. He figured they must be his grandmother when she'd been younger. In one of them, she was holding a little boy's hand. Benjy got a shock when he saw that the boy looked exactly like him. Then he realized it must be his father when he was a child. Miss Leota was holding the boy's hand firmly and had a strangely preoccupied expression on her face, but Benjy's father was smiling angelically for the camera.

Next to that picture was a wedding photograph. Benjy was sure that was his grandparents. Miss Leota was smiling at the camera in that one, her whole face happy. The man next to her must be his grandfather. He looked very stern, Benjy thought. He stood stiffly beside Miss Leota, holding her hand up proudly so that the photographer could catch her wedding ring sparkling, but his eyes were staring off into the distance.

Benjy turned away from the photographs. More familiar faces stared down at him from the walls. A slender man in a neat black suit studied Benjy sternly through the same clear blue eyes his father and Miss Leota shared. Beside him, another man with the same face, bearded this time, looked down at him from a Confederate uniform.

"Those are your ancestors."

Benjy jumped at the voice, and whirled around to find Miss Leota standing beside him.

"I'm sorry," he stammered. "I didn't mean to bother you. I didn't touch anything—I was just looking."

"I know that, Benjamin," Miss Leota told him. "They are your family, and you ought to know about them."

She led him into the center of the room and pointed to the painting of the man in the dark suit. "That was my father," she said. "His name was Edward also. I named your father after him. Actually, there was a twinkle in his eye that the artist failed to catch. Otherwise, it's quite a good likeness."

Benjy grinned, relieved. Somehow, his great-grandfather looked friendlier now that he knew about the twinkle.

"And that was his father," Miss Leota said, turning to the next painting.

"Did he fight in the War Between the States?" Benjy ventured.

"Of course he did," Miss Leota said promptly. "Every man and boy who could stand up fought for the cause. This is our land, and we have never tolerated strangers coming down here and trying to run our lives."

. Benjy studied the man in the Confederate uniform. That would be his great-great-grandfather, he calculated. Stumbling upon all this family history at once was a little awe inspiring.

"What do you think of your family?" Miss Leota asked abruptly, as though she were reading his thoughts. "Is it too much to handle all at once?"

Benjy considered this. "It's kind of nice," he said, discovering as he said it an unexpected sense of belonging deep inside. The feeling warmed him. Was this the way Hugh had wanted to feel, this sense of being part of a long line?

"Miss Leota," he asked suddenly, "why haven't we met you before?"

She took so long to answer, Benjy was afraid he had offended her. "I'm sorry," he stammered, clutching his book tightly and starting to back out of the room. He was just beginning to feel safe here—why had he gone and upset his grandmother?

"No," Miss Leota said, raising one hand imperiously to stop him. "It's quite all right, Benjamin. I don't mind your asking. I was just uncertain how to explain it to you."

She sighed. "As you might have suspected, your father and I did not get along at all well. Edward was my only son, and he could not wait to grow up, to get away from the South, to get away from me and from his father. And once he was gone, he refused to return.

"I suppose it might have been different if he had made a success of himself," she said sadly. "Then he could have come back in triumph to show us how right he had been. But that did not happen." She faced Benjy suddenly. "I'm sorry, Benjamin—I'm sure you love your father."

Benjy shrugged uncomfortably. He wasn't sure exactly what he felt for his father. How could you love someone who went off and dumped you? He didn't want to talk about love. "Why didn't he ever come back?" he asked.

"I'm sorry to say that your father had no patience," Miss Leota said. "If something did not come easily to him, he ran away from it and turned to something else. I'm afraid he ran away from me."

I guess he ran away from us too, Benjy thought. It made him feel a little better to think that they weren't the only people Edward Stark had run away from.

"Anyway," Miss Leota said, "when he left us, he never looked back. If your mother had not written to me privately, I would never have known that you and your sister existed."

"Mom wrote you?" Benjy asked, amazed. His mother was always so busy—he would never have imagined she'd take the trouble to write some unknown in-laws just to tell them about a couple of troublesome kids. Maybe there were a lot of things he hadn't realized about her. Maybe he and Fran were more important to her than he'd thought.

"She did." Miss Leota nodded. "When she told me your name especially, Benjamin, I felt very pleased. I thought perhaps your father did value his family heritage in some measure."

"Why?" Benjy asked.

"My grandfather's name was Benjamin," Miss Leota said quietly.

Benjy looked up at the portraits on the wall again. "The Confederate officer?" he asked hesitantly.

Miss Leota nodded. "Yes. Your father must have named you after him. I am sorry he left you and your mother and sister in the end, but I felt glad that he had given you a portion of your heritage first. Since then, I've been hoping for the opportunity to meet you and Frances, but I admit I was unsure how to go about it, and I allowed far too much time to elapse. When your mother suggested this brief trip to get acquainted, I couldn't have been more pleased."

"But Mom just wanted to go off on a vacation with her boyfriend," Benjy objected. Even as he spoke, he remembered her call and the postcard.

Miss Leota shot him a critical look. "Don't be so quick to judge other people, Benjamin. I expect your mother needed a holiday of her own. Everyone needs some time away."

Benjy shrugged. It was hard to understand other people "getting away" when he was always the one left behind.

"Don't confuse going off on a vacation with running away," Miss Leota said sharply. "Your mother will be home when you return from your visit here, and she will probably be in a much happier frame of mind after a little time to herself. As you will be," she pointed out.

Benjy thought about it. Getting off alone wasn't the same thing as running away, he knew that. His mother hadn't abandoned them the way his father had; she'd stayed there and supported them and tried her best. Maybe he'd been too ready to write her off because he was already hurt by his father's leaving, and he didn't want anybody else to hurt him like that. He might have made a mistake. People you cared about didn't have to hurt you. After all, he'd reached out to Miss Leota, and she hadn't hurt him.

"It's good to know you wanted us to come," Benjy told Miss Leota sincerely. "We weren't sure at first."

Miss Leota looked at her grandson, her face softening. "I couldn't be more pleased to have you here, Benjamin. I'm sorry I did not know how to show you that more clearly. I hope you'll come visit me often, now that we know each other."

Benjy looked up, his face glowing. "That would be wonderful!" he cried.

Miss Leota blushed slightly, as though his obvious delight was too much for her. She nodded at him, and started to leave the room. Then she thought better of it and turned back to him from the doorway. "I'm glad you like your ancestors, Benjamin. I believe they'd be proud of you."

Benjy watched her go, realizing that she was proud of him. That had to be a first. Smiling to himself, he turned back to the portraits. It made him feel strangely pleased that these men from the past, especially the Confederate officer with his name, would be proud of him also.

"You'll be even more proud of me soon, great-great-grandfather," he whispered, "when Hugh and I find that watch. We will, too! You'll see!"

☆ 11 ☆

HUGH'S STORY

Please don't let today be too late, Benjy begged Hugh silently as he ran across the dripping field to his culvert. The storm had stopped sometime in the night, and it was another clear, sunny spring morning. Only the drenched bushes and grass were evidence of the awful rain that had fallen the day before.

Benjy found a noisy little stream rushing through the concrete culvert. He had to edge along the side of it to miss the worst of the rainwater, but his sneakers were already so wet a little more dampness wasn't going to matter. On the other side of the interstate, Benjy skirted the downhill waterfall flowing toward the culvert's opening and hurried up to the wheelwright shop.

"Hugh!" he called softly. "I'm here, Hugh!"

"I missed you yesterday," Hugh's voice answered from behind him.

Benjy jumped slightly. "Why do you always come up

from behind like that?" he demanded, trying to cover his surprise.

Hugh shrugged. "You probably would not like the sensation if I just materialized in front of you," he said without much interest.

"Oh, I hadn't thought about that," Benjy said. He looked at the ghost with concern. "You're not mad I couldn't make it yesterday, are you?" he asked worriedly. "It was such a storm—if there were only somewhere indoors we could have met, we wouldn't have had to lose a day."

"That's all right," Hugh said dully. "One day matters little. There just isn't enough time." The Cadet sighed. "Tomorrow's the fourteenth, Ben. We're too late."

"That's not too late," Benjy told him. "I don't leave until the seventeenth, remember? That's four whole days from now. That's lots of time!"

Hugh shook his head. "Not for me. Unless we can find the watch today or tomorrow—" His voice trailed off mournfully.

"Did you come up with any new ideas about where to look?" Benjy asked, hoping to cheer his friend up.

But Hugh only shook his head again. "There's nowhere left," he said unhappily.

"Sometimes, Ben," he said softly, "I just cannot understand how this all happened. I never wanted to come to VMI—I was at Hillsboro Military Academy near home, and it was all right. At least I was used to it. But my mother got the idea into her head that I'd be safer at VMI because the Institute Cadets had never been called on to participate in the War, so she insisted I come here.

"But I was miserable at first." Hugh frowned, painfully remembering. "The others laughed at me—they looked down on me because I wasn't a Virginian. And I had never been so far from North Carolina before— I couldn't understand why my father was so eager for me to go. Once it came time for me to leave, my mother changed her mind and raised all manner of objections and prayed that I would not go through with it. She even wrote the colonel here to tell him I must be late because I had twisted my ankle. A twisted ankle, honestly! But my father got me on the road all right only a little behind schedule. And my grandfather was there with the watch. . . ."

Hugh smiled distantly at the memory. "Then, once I grew accustomed to the Institute, things seemed to get better. I really liked being on my own, away from home, without my mother deciding everything for me. And once the other Cadets got to know me, they became friendlier also. I was beginning to think I had found someplace that was all my own, someplace where I belonged, for myself."

He grinned. "For the first time in my life I had friends who treated me as an equal, and who called me Hugh instead of Willie." He grimaced at the baby

name. "And as we all worked together and drilled together, they came to accept me as me."

Benjy nodded. He knew exactly what Hugh meant
about wanting to belong just for his own sake. And he
knew how good it could feel. Hugh and Miss Leota
were the first people who had ever accepted him, and
he didn't know how he was going to tear himself away
from them to go home in four days.

"By that May," Hugh was saying, "I truly believed I
had a future in the Corps, and then in the Army. And
when they called us out, I felt so good about fighting
at New Market. I was so glad my father had stood up
for my coming to VMI—I was sure he'd be proud of
me. I knew my mother would faint when she heard
the news that I'd gone into battle, but there was nothing she could do to prevent me."

Hugh looked up at Benjy, his face shining. "I believed going to battle with my friends would finally set
me free, and make me a man at last instead of a mam-
ma's boy. I was done with hiding behind my mother,
with asking her to take care of things for me. I was
ready to be responsible for my own life, and for my
homeland, and for the lives of my friends."

Then his face fell. "But I failed there, too. All I did
was get killed. I didn't do any good, I didn't even get
a chance to fire my musket once at those damn Yankees! All I did was fall down in the mud and lose the
family watch." He shook his head. "I would swear my

father was bitterly angry about that. He could have salvaged the watch even if he couldn't salvage me."

Hugh's eyes met Benjy's longingly. "At least my grandfather believed I could make something of myself. Even if it didn't do any good in the end, he must have believed it might work—at least he wanted me to get away and try. Don't you think he believed in me?" he asked.

"I'm sure he did," Benjy said, understanding how badly Hugh needed to be reassured. "And even if your father was angry about the watch, I bet your grandfather understood."

"Maybe," Hugh said, unconvinced. "But perhaps he thought in the end I was just a failure."

"You weren't a failure!" Benjy cried. "You made it to the battle, you fought! I've never done anything in my whole life as brave as go to battle for my family or my country, but you did! And the rest of the Corps—they don't think you failed. Every year they have a ceremony at VMI honoring all ten of you who died—I read about it in a history book! There's a parade and a roll call and everything! That should show you they're proud of you. And it should make you ashamed of yourself for thinking you're a failure. Doesn't it make you feel proud inside to see them honoring you?"

"I cannot see it," Hugh muttered. "I am never able to attend the ceremony. It's a great moment for the others—they march around and recall how brave they were and feel true Confederate pride—but I am bound to this battlefield until my family knows the truth about my watch. All I can do, year after year, is get shot again and again, and fumble about trying to protect my watch and die—and all that keeps going through my head is how stupid I was!"

"Again?" Benjy repeated. His voice dropped to a whisper. "You can only die once, Hugh," he said unsteadily. "That was a long time ago."

Hugh shook his head. He was twisting his gray cap between his hands. "Remember, I said you'd be here for the battle?" he asked.

Benjy nodded, his eyes wide.

"Every year," Hugh told him in a low, steady voice, "the call is sounded. The bugles blow, General Breckinridge needs us, and we march into New Market and plug the hole in the Confederate line again. Every year, we march across this wheat field to those farmhouses, and every year I go forward, telling myself perhaps it will happen differently this time. But every year it's all the same."

Hugh shut his eyes tight, seeing the battle yet again. "I feel the musket ball, and it's like somebody punches me in the chest and all the air is knocked out of me. I can feel nothing at all, and I'm falling, and I cannot seem to draw any air into my lungs. And suddenly the ground strikes me in the back and I start breathing again. Then the pain starts."

Hugh twisted his cap violently, as though he were fighting the pain again. "It hurts, almost like a terrible burn, but it's worse than a burn—my whole chest is on fire, like the pain is just eating me up, and all I can think of is that watch—what will happen to my grandfather's watch?

"The rest of the Corps is marching past me. I can see them, but I can't hear their boots in the mud, or the yells at the front line, or even the guns. And then all of a sudden the pain isn't there anymore, and I can feel the muddy, broken wheat stalks underneath me and the rain on my face, and I know I have to keep breathing long enough to take care of the watch."

Hugh's face took on a fixed, determined expression. "I roll over and make myself crawl, just trying to keep breathing, and I pray the pain will not come back, and then—there it is in front of me! I see this crack, and I know that it is big enough. It is a black emptiness between some stones, I cannot see more clearly than that. Everything is growing darker around me, and I know I must hurry. I crawl right up to that crack, and I reach for the watch.

"I can hardly make my fingers work anymore, they feel so numb, but I tear open the front of my tunic and pull the watch out, and I manage to get hold of the rag I carry with my musket and I wrap it around the watch. The oil will keep it clean, I'm thinking." Hugh smiled a little. "It is a miracle how clearly I keep thinking. Then I reach in and push it as far into the crack as it will go. With the dirty rag around it, you can't even see there's anything hidden in there."

Hugh sighed deeply and leaned his head back, smiling that strange, otherworldly smile Benjy remembered so well from their first meeting. "So I know the watch is safe, and I roll back on the mud and try to look up. I can feel the rain, softly now, but I can no longer see the sky. It's too far away, and everything is too dark. And I lie there telling myself everything is all right now, I've done my job. I can almost see my grandfather, nodding at me, and I tell him his watch is safe from the Yankees. And my father is smiling, and I say, see, I am a true McDowell, you can be proud of me now."

Suddenly Hugh stopped smiling. His head snapped down, and his face was twisted. "Only it's all a lie, don't you see? I did nothing right, and they weren't proud of me! I'm dishonored! Despite my best efforts to preserve it, I lost a family heirloom, and there's nothing I can do about it, not ever! I can't even take part in our roll call at VMI on the fifteenth, not until the watch is restored and I can show that I deserve the honor the rest of the Cadets are due. I must recover that watch, Ben, and get it back to the McDowells so that history will be corrected and my family will know how much I valued our honor," he said desperately. "Otherwise I'll be condemned to remain in disgrace on this battlefield forever!"

"No, you won't," Benjy heard himself saying. His

voice was terribly calm. An idea had been forming in the back of his mind, and as much as it terrified him, he knew it was their only answer.

"You said I'd be here for the battle, didn't you?" Benjy went on, trying to concentrate on what finding the watch meant to Hugh and to ignore what his suggestion could mean to him. Benjy's voice faltered at the risks his plan would entail, but he made himself go on. "I'll come to the battle, Hugh, and I'll look closely while you hide your watch. Once I know where it is, I can take it out for you and bring it back to VMI so they can find your family. Then you'll be free of this battlefield, and you can come to the ceremony with your friends and rest in peace afterward."

"Come to the battle?" Hugh whispered. "No living person has ever seen our battle before, in all these years."

"No one has ever seen you before, either," Benjy pointed out, trying to sound braver than he felt.

"But—it is not a night for the living. What if you cannot get out of it?" Hugh asked softly, putting into words the fear Benjy had been trying to ignore. "What if you are trapped with me forever?"

Benjy swallowed. "That's a chance I'll have to take."

☆ 12 ☆

LAST-MINUTE FEARS

"**Y**ou've been exceptionally quiet today," Miss Leota commented, coming into the living room where Benjy sat curled up in a large armchair. "You haven't even been out to the battlefield."

Benjy looked up from the book on Stonewall Jackson. He had been staring at the pages, but he hadn't been able to concentrate. "I'm just kind of tired, I guess," he told his grandmother.

"Tired?" she asked, eying him critically. Benjy suddenly remembered the gaping hole in the toes of his left sock and squirmed into the armchair cushions, trying to hide the sock before she noticed it.

"I hope you're not coming down with something," was all she said, however. "After all your interest, it would be a pity if you missed the New Market ceremony tomorrow."

Stunned, Benjy blinked up at her. Then he realized she must be talking about the annual celebration of the battle's anniversary, the fancy parade at VMI and everything. For a minute, he had thought she knew about the ghostly battle that would take place tonight.

He had been trying not to think about his promise to Hugh. It had been his own idea, and Benjy wasn't sorry he had come up with it, but the thought of being in the battlefield in the midst of an army of ghosts frightened him far more than climbing down the roof in the dark had.

"I'll be driving to VMI tomorrow to pick up some research materials from the Marshall Library and to attend the ceremony honoring the New Market Cadets," Miss Leota was saying. "If you would like to come along, I'll be happy to take you."

Benjy wondered if he'd be in any condition to drive to VMI with his grandmother tomorrow. What if he were still trapped in some ghostly limbo? Then he pushed the treacherous thought out of his mind and tried to smile up at the white-haired lady studying him. "I'd like to see that, Miss Leota," he stammered, "if I wouldn't be in your way or anything. I've read about the dress parade and calling the roll of the Cadets who died and everything."

"You certainly won't be in the way," Miss Leota assured him. "In fact, Fran will be coming also. She's mentioned something about some Cadet who will be participating in the ceremony. She's eager to introduce him to me. Apparently he turned out to be a young gentleman after all and forgave her for not coming to visit the other evening."

Benjy couldn't help laughing. "Maybe she's turning over a new leaf, Miss Leota."

"Perhaps." Miss Leota smiled. "I thought we'd leave at ten o'clock. That will get us there before the tourists and in time for my appointment at the library."

Benjy nodded. "That sounds good."

His grandmother started back to her office, then turned back. "Are you quite sure you're all right, Benjamin?" she asked again. Her voice sounded worried, and Benjy could see deep lines of concern in the frown across her forehead.

He wanted to give her a genuine smile. It felt good to know Miss Leota was sincerely concerned about him. But he was so scared about the coming night, he just couldn't seem to act natural. And he couldn't tell Miss Leota about going to the ghosts' battle—she'd think he was crazy! Even if he considered the remote possibility that she might believe him, Benjy was certain she'd never let him go for fear something would happen to him. That was exactly what Benjy was afraid of himself, but he'd given his word. He kept telling himself he had to be there.

"I'll be fine," he told her, hoping she'd understand just how much her caring meant to him, even though he didn't know how to say it.

She smiled at him from the doorway, the softer wrinkles around her eyes crinkling warmly. To Benjy, even across the room, it felt as good as an unhurried, thorough hug, and all of a sudden he discovered he was able to forget the coming battle long enough to smile back at her.

Then she was gone, and Benjy returned to his book with a sigh. He had tried reading in his bedroom earlier, but he couldn't help looking at the cemetery and thinking of Hugh, and then his imagination would take over and start conjuring up all sorts of images of what was going to happen. Those scenes of ghostly soldiers and blood-soaked battlefields hadn't made him feel any better at all. Down here in the living room it was harder to believe in that sort of ghost, and Benjy felt a little safer.

"Well, well," Fran's teasing voice interrupted his worries. "What's this? I thought you'd moved into that stupid battlefield permanently, Benjy—what are you doing moping around the house?"

Benjy shrugged, hoping she was on her way out. Sometimes, if she was in a big hurry, she didn't feel like wasting much time picking on him.

"Reading," Fran answered her own question. She stared down at him, shaking her head. "Honestly, Benjy, you're so boring—don't you just bore yourself to death? Reading all the time and making up imaginary friends—"

"Shut up," Benjy said angrily. For a second he felt

the old urge to throw something at her, but the idea felt uncomfortable. Instead he glared at his sister through narrowed eyes and said coldly, "I don't have any imaginary friends, and I am not even remotely bored with anything right now. In fact, I've got more things going on than I know what to do about, and I'd appreciate it if you'd mind your own business and let me take care of myself, okay?"

He saw Fran's eyes widen in surprise, and knew that that speech didn't sound anything like the little brother she was used to. Benjy realized he'd made it so easy for her to make him lose his temper and look dumb that she'd gotten in the habit of teasing him without even thinking about it anymore. She had just taken for granted that was the only way to treat him.

"Well!" she said, trying to sound insulted. But her voice rang hollow. "Pardon me, Benjamin Stark! I was just going to tell you that if you're coming with Miss Leota and me to VMI to meet Robert tomorrow, you'd better make yourself presentable. I'm not about to be embarrassed by some grubby little brother." And she turned regally, flipping her long hair back toward him, and strode out of the living room.

Benjy listened to her footsteps echo down the hallway to the side door. He felt pleased with himself. When was the last time he had stood up to Fran without crying or flying into some sort of violent rage? He couldn't remember. Had he ever tried it before?

It must have been that crack about imaginary friends. Hugh was real, all right. He might be a ghost, but he was very real, and whatever happened tonight was going to be real, too. No matter how afraid Benjy was, he knew that the VMI Cadets, deep down inside, must have been much more frightened the day they marched into Yankee cannon fire to take their position in the front line for the Confederacy. And yet they'd done their job, every one of them.

Benjy remembered the pinched look of misery on Hugh's face. He knew how important that watch was to Hugh. How could he compare his fears to the fears of the VMI Cadets? And with Hugh's honor hanging in the balance, what were his fears worth anyway? Whatever happened, he would be there tonight, and he knew he wouldn't come home without the watch.

Then he grinned to himself. He'd have to stand up to Fran more often. After all, what could she do to him for sticking up for himself? She couldn't be any meaner to him than she already was, and maybe she'd be nicer if he didn't let her get away with being obnoxious all the time. He'd have to remember that. Benjy sighed, feeling serious again. One thing about this vacation— he certainly was learning he could do a lot of things he'd never imagined before.

Somehow, the afternoon dissolved into evening, and Benjy left his unread book to help set the table for supper. Fran was quiet during the meal, but Benjy hardly noticed. He guessed she was giving him a wide berth after his sharpness this afternoon, although her backing down from him so easily did seem uncharacteristic. But his mind was too full to worry about her.

He scarcely even noticed Miss Leota, who kept trying to get his attention all during the meal. But he just wasn't thinking about Stonewall Jackson or the Valley campaigns, and the best he could manage were yeses and nos and shrugs in response to her questions. He was thinking about a very real battle that was about to take place in a matter of hours, and nothing else mattered.

Benjy hurried to help clear things away after supper, then he retreated to his bedroom. It was twilight outside, and he stood looking at the cemetery as the light disappeared. He remembered Hugh's haunting singing the first night he had arrived. If he hadn't heard Hugh that night, would any of this have happened?

He decided it was a silly thought. He and Hugh were bound together in this; they were always meant to be friends and to do for each other what no one else could have done. All he had to do was tiptoe downstairs after it grew completely dark, slip onto the battlefield, watch until the bitter end, and then recover the McDowell family watch. Then it would be finished.

Only one thought nagged at the back of Benjy's mind. If the bonds of friendship between him and Hugh held the two of them so close together, what would happen to him after Hugh died in the battle tonight?

☆ **13** ☆

THE BATTLE OF NEW MARKET

After Miss Leota retired to her office and Fran shut herself in her bedroom, Benjy got ready to leave. He hung the flashlight on his belt again and slipped his rusty knife into his pocket. He wished he'd gotten a whetstone and sharpened it so he could show Hugh that he'd learned something. Tomorrow he'd have to remember to ask Miss Leota where he could get a whetstone. Taking care of that knife properly, like Hugh would, suddenly seemed terribly important.

He pulled on his denim jacket and slowly snapped it up. Finally, he bent down and untied his sneakers. He tucked them under one arm, turned off his room light, and quietly pushed the door open a crack. There was no sound coming out of Fran's room, so he shut the door quietly and tiptoed uncomfortably to the top of the staircase.

Benjy hadn't decided what to do if Miss Leota caught him sneaking out of the house. He hadn't wasted much energy worrying about it. He was counting on his stocking feet being too quiet to disturb her. Maybe he really did hope she'd hear him, he admitted to himself as he leaned over the rail to look at her office door. Then she might stop him, and he could quit worrying about being a part of the battle that was about to occur.

Despite his fears, Benjy inched his way down the stairs, keeping an eye on Miss Leota's door. He made it into the hallway without being discovered. In the little room by the side door, he sat down and put his shoes on again, tying the laces very slowly. Now there was no way he could stay in his room and claim he'd been prevented from keeping his word to Hugh, no matter how afraid he was to face an army of ghosts on the battlefield. Would they be able to tell the difference between him and the Yankees they were fighting? Benjy shuddered at the thought. And what happened to you if a ghostly bullet struck you?

Benjy felt a profound urge to run upstairs and hide in his room until morning. The old Benjy would have done just that, but as much as the whole idea frightened him, the new Benjy had given his word to his friend, and he couldn't bring himself to run away. Benjy had never managed to do anything right before, but he'd never had the chance to do anything special, either. And this was truly important, both to Hugh and to himself. Hugh had been brave; he hadn't run away from the battle. And even after he had been shot, he hadn't just rolled over and died. He'd struggled forward to hide the watch safely. If Hugh could be brave and do things even if they were hard, then Benjy could also. Benjy wasn't going to run away like his father.

He let himself out of the house and took off for the battlefield at a steady trot. He wasn't interested any longer in excuses to prevent him from meeting Hugh tonight. Even though he was still afraid, he knew he wanted to be at the battlefield, beside his friend. He was determined to do his job right. He swung himself over the woven wire fence and kept up his pace through the rocky field until he reached the culvert. It was darker than it had been the other night, when he and Hugh had first tried to find the watch, and the shadows were even thicker in the concrete tunnel. Benjy paused, wondering exactly what he'd find on the other side. Would the armies already be in position? Would he see them?

Would they see him?

But even the culvert couldn't stop Benjy that night. He would keep his word and see the battle through. He would not go home without the watch.

Taking a deep breath, Benjy clenched his fists and hurtled through the culvert. Pulling himself up on the other side, he ordered his imagination to stop tormenting him and made himself look around. In the darkness, the battlefield looked the same as it had the day before. The grass was still damp from the rain, and Benjy could clearly see the freshly dug earth packed back into the trough he had gouged out around the blacksmith shop with the mattock. Nothing had changed. Where was the battle?

"You came!"

Hugh's voice sounded amazed.

"Yeah," Benjy admitted, relieved to see his friend. "I wasn't sure I'd be here either. This is kind of scary, Hugh—what's going to happen?"

Hugh tried to smile back, but his voice shook. "Only the battle," he said.

Benjy shrugged. "So, where is everybody?" he asked, keeping his voice light.

Hugh pointed away from the farm buildings. "We're in reserve back there, waiting to be called up. I have to get back into position now or I'll be in trouble. But I wanted to be here to meet you."

"Is it time already?" Benjy stammered, suddenly afraid for real. What would a battle be like?

"Almost," Hugh said.

"Well, where should I be?" Benjy demanded, looking around. "I mean, I don't want to be in the way or anything."

"I don't know," the Cadet said uncertainly. "We'll cross this field, but you'll see us coming. Stay back from our line. And watch for me—I'll be in the company just to the right of the colors."

Benjy nodded.

"Listen, Ben," the other boy said unsteadily, "give me your word?"

"Sure," Benjy told him.

"When—when it happens, when you're watching me hide the watch," Hugh said in a trembling voice, "please—don't think worse of me because I've failed to find the watch since then. I've told you how it happened—I did try my best, Ben, I was dying, and the world seemed so dark—I couldn't see beyond the crack—"

"Don't worry," Benjy said uncomfortably. "I know you, Hugh, I know you're all right. You're my friend."

The Cadet stared down at his boots and scuffed them in the dirt. "Just don't wish you'd never met me," he whispered. "I'll never forget you."

Both boys jumped at the distant sound of a bugle.

"I must go!" Hugh looked once more at Benjy, his expression a blend of hope and desperation. "You're a true friend, Ben, I—I appreciate your being here tonight. Please find the watch for me!"

"I'll find it," Benjy promised, but his friend was already gone, running across the field to join his comrades.

A drop of rain suddenly hit Benjy on the head. He looked up at the sky, surprised. There had been no rain clouds overhead when he'd started out. Now it seemed hazy, and rain was definitely falling. Benjy shivered, feeling more miserable than ever. He looked around, wondering what was happening with the battle.

Very faintly, Benjy heard a dull roar. He turned uphill, toward the sound. There it was again. It must be the cars on the interstate, he told himself, and glanced at the freeway. To his astonishment, he could scarcely see it. He could make out a shadowy shape hanging over the battlefield, but as hard as he squinted he couldn't bring it into focus. The roar was getting louder. Was it gunfire?

Benjy strained to see up toward the cannon. Was he hearing the Union guns firing at the Confederates? And what were those shadowy figures he could almost make out through the rain, running by the farm buildings? They were men, running toward him!

Benjy felt real panic and whirled around, trying to think where to run. Then he saw neat, orderly lines of soldiers marching toward him from the rear. They were in sharper focus than anything else he'd seen that night, and he recognized the gray uniforms and flat caps right away. This was the Corps of Cadets, marching into place to fill the hole in the line. Those other figures he had seen running must have been the men of the Second Brigade who'd fallen back. But everything would be all right now; the Cadets would do their job. And Hugh was somewhere among them!

Benjy staggered backward, remembering he was supposed to stay out of the way of the Corps. Tall, soft things brushed his knees, and he looked down, startled. It had been a wheat field in 1864, he remembered. Benjy stared at the ghostly wheat, confused. Had he stumbled into 1864, or had the ghosts brought their world to him? Both past and present seemed shadowy and unreal.

The Corps of Cadets kept marching forward. Benjy could see them sharply now, almost as clearly as he usually saw Hugh. They marched in perfect step, oblivious to the rain, striding through the broken stalks of wheat, carrying their long, awkward muskets at the ready. In the middle, surrounded by the color guard, one tall Cadet proudly carried a white-and-gold flag up high.

The gunfire was growing louder. The Cadets never faltered, their faces set and determined. If they'd been excited earlier, it was hard to see now. And if they'd been afraid before they started, Benjy could see no trace of fear on their faces as they marched toward the guns.

But where was Hugh?

Suddenly a shell crashed in the middle of the marching Cadets. A hole appeared in the formation as the shell exploded. Benjy cried out as he saw the lifeless forms of two fallen Cadets. A third struggled on the ground, his fingers digging frantically at the rain-soaked ground as though he could hold onto life if he could only get a tight enough hold on the earth.

Without pause, the remaining Cadets marched on.

A voice rang out, "Close ranks!" and the line tightened up until Benjy couldn't see the empty space where the three Cadets had been. A few Cadets in the rear of the formation looked down at their fallen friends as they marched around their bodies. Benjy couldn't make out the expression in the Cadets' eyes—was it sorrow for their comrades' deaths, or pride for their having given their best?

Benjy wildly scanned the passing line of Cadets for Hugh. Where could his friend be? How would Benjy know when Hugh was about to get hit? Benjy thought of the three Cadets he'd already seen die, and tried to block the image of their broken bodies out of his head. They were already dead, he tried to tell himself—they were ghosts! But for him, as for the ghosts marching bravely into battle, this moment was all the reality there was.

Suddenly Benjy caught sight of a familiar figure. Shorter than the other Cadets protecting the colors, holding his head high and marching forward in step with his comrades, Hugh was headed straight toward the shop building they had first dug around. Benjy caught his breath. Why had Hugh been afraid Benjy would look down on him after the battle? Cadet Private William Hugh McDowell was marching forward, every inch a soldier. There was no trace of fear on his face, even though the ghost knew what was going to happen. Benjy felt proud of his friend as he watched him advance with the Corps. Even Hugh's father would have been proud of his son if he had seen him at this moment, Benjy felt sure of that.

Then Hugh staggered.

"No!" Benjy screamed, but he knew it was too late.

Hugh pitched backward, croaking for breath, his arms flung up in the air, still gripping his musket. He fell backward, his sodden cap tumbling off into the wheat. Around him the other Cadets marched forward, closing their ranks once again. Hugh's body arched as it hit the ground, and then Benjy could see his chest heave and knew his friend was breathing again.

"Don't die," Benjy whispered, even though he knew the words were useless. Hugh was already dead. Only his ghost was playing out these last few terrible moments in the desperate hope that its spirit would finally be given rest. This has to count for something, Benjy thought. He rubbed his jacket sleeve roughly against his eyes so he could see without the tears getting in the way.

Hugh was dragging himself along the ground. The other Cadets had already reached the farm buildings and were getting into position along the fence on the far side. Benjy forced himself to watch each agonizing inch of Hugh's progress, trying to help his friend forward with the force of his own thoughts. Hugh doggedly crawled toward the wheelwright shop, still clutching his musket in one hand.

"Drop the stupid old gun," Benjy muttered, but he knew that was no use. Hugh cared about things. He wouldn't throw away his musket any more than he'd let his watch be stolen. Even if it cost him a few extra moments of life, he wouldn't leave it behind.

Then Hugh was at the building. He nearly banged into it, crawling forward blindly until there was no more space to crawl. Oblivious to the battle raging around them, Benjy crept forward to see. Hugh lay motionless, staring straight ahead at the stone foundation of the building directly in front of him. The crack!

Benjy saw it too, a clear crack between the uneven rocks. How could they have missed it earlier? He jumped back suddenly as Hugh rolled over heavily onto his back. The Cadet's face was lined with dirt from his slow progress through the muddy wheat field. His breathing came in jerks. Benjy thought he saw blood at the corner of his friend's mouth. Then Hugh groped at the collar of his tunic. Weakly, he fumbled at the buttons near the top, then tore impatiently at the collar. Benjy ached to reach out and help him, but he kept back. Hugh had to do this himself. Benjy's job would come later.

Finally the tunic tore. Hugh shoved it back and reached unsteadily into the inner pocket for his watch. He pulled it out, and held it near his eyes for a moment. He pressed the clasp and opened the watch, peering at the inside of the gold lid, trying hard to read

the loving inscription one last time. Then he closed it
and let his left hand fall onto his chest, still clutching
the watch, while his right hand blundered down into
his pouch of ammunition and supplies. He managed to
pull out an oily rag, which he wrapped around the
watch, carefully tucking all the corners in despite his
numb fingers.

Hugh rolled over onto his side awkwardly, his wet
hair falling across his forehead. He reached weakly forward until he found the crack in the foundation, and
he shoved the watch inside. Then he fell onto his back,
a sigh of relief on his lips.

Benjy watched his friend's face relax. The rain had
washed away most of the dirt by now. Hugh looked
younger, and almost happy as he lay there. Was he
seeing his grandfather and his father? Benjy didn't know
for sure, but he had to tell Hugh everything was fine.
He crept to the side of the dying Cadet and reached
out a hand to brush the hair off of his face. He could
barely feel the ghost now, but he saw the hair move
under his fingers.

"I know where the watch is now, Hugh," Benjy said
softly, trying to keep his own misery out of his voice.
"You found a good place for it. Don't feel bad, Hugh,
you did everything you should have done. Your friends
know that, and I'm sure your grandfather knows. I hope
your father realizes it."

Hugh lay quietly, his chest heaving less and less fre-
quently. His face was peaceful. Benjy thought he could

see a smile playing about the corners of Hugh's mouth. He hoped the Cadet could hear him.

"And you know what was best of all, Hugh?" Benjy went on. "You were a good friend to me. I really needed a friend, and you did a great job. I'll never have another friend as good as you."

Hugh sighed, and Benjy realized his friend was dead. A thread of blood ran out of the corner of Hugh's mouth, but the rain flowed over it until the boy's face looked serene and unmarked again.

"No," Benjy said, backing away. "No—not yet!"

Had Hugh even heard him? Would he be at peace now, certain that things were going to be all right? How could he go off and leave Benjy without telling him these things?

"It's not fair!" Benjy shouted.

He tried to block out the sound of the gunfire and the yells of the men at the front. He tried to tune them all out and to make his mind go blank the way he used to, but it didn't work this time. Benjy didn't think it would ever work again. He'd made the decision to face up to facts with Hugh, and to accept the responsibility of doing something about them. He couldn't ever go back to being a helpless baby. No matter how much it hurt, he had to face up to the fact that the battle was still there and Hugh's dead body lay in front of him. None of it was going to go away just because he didn't like it.

All along Benjy had known this was what had happened. When he'd read Miss Leota's book, he'd known William Hugh McDowell died at the battle. Knowing his friend was a ghost should have meant admitting that Hugh really had died—but somehow none of that had brought home the reality of death to Benjy the way the body lying beside the shop building did.

Hugh was his first true friend, the first person who had believed in him and needed him, and now Hugh was dead. Benjy fell on the ground beside Hugh's body and wept angry, bitter tears that burned his eyes. What happens after a ghost dies? Would he ever see Hugh again, ever laugh with him or plan with him? Would the two of them ever rejoice together over the recovered watch?

"Who's—oh, sorry, Mister." A passing soldier tipped his cap to Benjy, or to whomever he saw mourning a comrade's death, and hurried on his way. Was he hurrying forward to the battle or was the battle over by now, Benjy wondered vaguely. He knew the Confederates had won—why did Hugh have to die all over again? Benjy needed him.

Huddled by Hugh's stiffening body, Benjy cried the tears he'd never cried when his father had gone off, when his sister had turned on him, when his mother had been too busy to understand. He cried because he had just discovered that people would always leave— they'd die or they'd move on—but sooner or later they'd have to find their own way through their own lives and that would mean leaving him. Like it or not, he would have to accept it. And sometimes reaching out to people could work—Miss Leota had accepted his friendship, more than friendship, really. The two of them had grown to love each other.

Benjy had grown to love Hugh too, but Hugh was gone now, secure in the knowledge that he'd given his life for the best, truest cause, and trusting that Benjy would see his family's honor restored. And Edward Stark was gone also, tying to find some sort of success on his own, somewhere off without his son. It had been his decision, and Benjy didn't have to like it, but he had to accept it, the way he would have to accept his mother's growing relationship with Andy. Benjy would have to make his own way through his own life too.

The tears drying on his face, Benjy found himself kneeling by the rail fence beside the shop building. The night air was cool and dry around him. Where had the rain gone? Benjy looked around uncertainly. Now he could see the lights of the cars on the interstate, clear and sharp once again. The battle had returned to the past.

Benjy looked down at the ground—Hugh's body had disappeared. But Benjy could still see Hugh's dying attempt to protect the watch, and he knew Hugh still needed his help. Wearily, Benjy turned to the stone foundation.

But the crack had disappeared! Nothing looked the same, but Benjy knew he had seen the crack when Hugh had placed the watch inside. He dug out his knife and scraped at the dirt furiously, until he had hollowed out some space around the stones where Hugh had reached. Then he pulled out his flashlight and shone it onto the foundation.

There—Benjy clearly recognized the shape of the stones he had seen earlier. But there was no crack between them! He knew it had to be there; it couldn't have just disappeared!

Benjy bent down to look closer. To his surprise he saw that something had been spread across the uneven face of the foundation stones, sealing over the loose spaces—some sort of cement. He dug at it experimentally with one finger, but even though the edges flaked slightly, he couldn't pry the whole patch out. Benjy grabbed at his knife, fumbled open the largest blade, and then forced the knife blade behind the edge of the cement. He worked the blade back and forth, loosening the crumbly patch. Suddenly it broke free, and Benjy pried it out, leaving the stones just as they had been in 1864.

With trembling fingers, he reached into the crack, inching his fingers back until he felt a stiff fold of something—could it be the rag Hugh had wrapped the watch in? Trying not to get his hopes up, Benjy managed to get a firm grip on the object and carefully drew it out. It was a small, cloth-wrapped bundle!

Shakily, Benjy forced the stiff folds of cloth apart to reveal an aged gold watch. He pushed the catch and opened it slowly, holding his breath, and shone the flashlight on the inner lid. In the dim beam of light he could read the engraved names:

HUGH ROBERT MCDOWELL
1843
WILLIAM HUGH MCDOWELL
V M I 1867

☆ **14** ☆

THE RACE TO VMI

The sun streaming through the corner windows finally woke Benjy the next morning. He blinked at it and lay limply under the covers, wondering where he was. He must have dragged himself home last night, or was it this morning?

What had he done with the watch?

Benjy tried to sit upright in panic before he noticed his left hand was caught underneath his pillow. He drew it out slowly, and breathed a sigh of relief. He was still clutching Hugh's watch, carefully rewrapped in the same cloth Hugh had used originally. Forgetting his weariness, Benjy sat up and folded back the cloth eagerly.

In the morning sunlight, the gold gleamed brightly at him. He opened the watch carefully and read the inscriptions again. This was it, at last!

Benjy wanted to shout with delight and turn cartwheels around his room. He, Benjamin Stark, had actually gone into a ghost world to help his friend recover the precious family heirloom that had been lost for over a hundred years! That was better than hitting a home run or catching a touchdown pass or any of the other things he'd never been able to do. He felt as though he could do anything in the world! He was ready to burst with excitement—he wanted to celebrate with someone.

That thought made Benjy sit back, suddenly worried. The someone he wanted was Hugh. But what had happened to Hugh's ghost? That terrible scene on the rain-drenched wheat field sprang vividly into Benjy's mind. Benjy was afraid that witnessing his friend's death in the battle had changed everything. What if Hugh was now gone for good?

Benjy had to find out. He hurried into his clothes and shoved the watch securely into his jeans pocket. Then he charged out of his room.

"Hey, Benjy, where are you going?" Fran called as he rushed past.

"Over to the battlefield," Benjy said briefly.

"What's the big deal about that battlefield, anyway?" Fran demanded. "Don't you remember the ceremony at VMI? Miss Leota said we'd be leaving soon."

Something in her voice made Benjy hesitate at the top of the stairs and glance back at her. She was wearing a new soft green dress. He couldn't decide if she just sounded bossy like usual or if it was something else.

"You look really pretty," he said.

Fran smiled suddenly. "Miss Leota helped me pick this dress out yesterday. Can you believe there are some really neat clothes shops in town?"

Benjy grinned and answered her thought. "I'm not surprised—Miss Leota's okay, isn't she?"

"She really is. You know—I'm actually glad we came."

Benjy nodded, his hand tight around the watch in his pocket. "Yeah, me too." He started down the stairs.

"Benjy!" That odd note in Fran's voice was back, almost as if she needed something from him. "You can't go now—what about the ceremony at VMI?"

"I have to do something before I go, Fran," he told her. "Don't worry, I'll be back soon."

"Miss Leota said we'd be leaving at ten o'clock—if you're not ready, she'll leave you!"

Benjy was now positive that Fran needed him for something. He just couldn't imagine what. And he couldn't hang around waiting to find out. It was too important that he make sure everything was all right.

"Well, don't let her leave without me," he told his sister. "I'll run all the way."

"But Robert wanted to meet my family!" Fran wailed.

So that was it. Benjy hid a smile as he turned back to her. "Don't worry, I'll be back in time. And between Miss Leota and me, you'll do okay in the family department."

"Darn it, Benjy, can't you just forget about your battlefield for once? This matters to me!" Fran snapped, glaring at him. "Honestly, you ought to be grateful I even want to include you in this!"

Benjy watched her play nervously with her long hair. Fran was right—just last week, in fact, he would have been overjoyed if she'd wanted to include him in anything at all. But things had changed, and Benjamin Stark just wasn't the same person anymore. He had a friend, and he had something really important he had to take care of. He had responsibilities.

All the same, Fran was his sister.

"Look, I'm sorry, Fran," he said, "but it's really important that I see Hugh McDowell before I go. I promise I'll hurry back."

"What did you say?" Fran called after him as he ran down the last of the stairs and into the hall. "See who? Benjy, come back here!"

In the bright sunlight, Benjy could hardly believe how much the battlefield had changed. The streaming rain and the pounding shells and the charge of the Cadets still seemed so real to him, he'd half expected to see it all again today—the rain-drenched bodies drying stiffly in the sun, the blood-soaked mud slowly hardening. But it was all grass and neat gravel paths again— nothing like he remembered.

No wonder Hugh hadn't been able to find his watch here, Benjy thought. It wasn't the same at all. Even the trees and rocks seemed to have changed; old trees had fallen, perhaps, and new ones grown. The effect was as though nature itself had moved through the motions of some slow-paced dance to change its features so completely that no one would ever recognize its past face.

"Hugh?" Benjy called tentatively. He wasn't sure how to summon the ghost. Since they had become friends, Hugh had just turned up in his own good time as soon as he knew Benjy was there. But that was before Benjy had watched him die. Would Hugh still come, after the battle?

Benjy slumped against one of the trees and slid to the ground. How could it all be over? He'd tried so hard to help Hugh, and now he even had the watch— he had to be sure that everything had turned out all right. He couldn't just go home in a couple of days and never know.

Suddenly Benjy remembered Fran waiting for him. He'd forgotten his own watch in the excitement that morning. Was it ten o'clock yet? He remembered Hugh telling him about the ghostly roll call that the original New Market Cadets held while the modern Corps held their own ceremony. If he went with Fran and Miss Leota and they got to VMI early enough, and if he could find out anything about the remaining McDowell family before the ceremony, maybe Hugh would be set free from the battlefield and would be able to join the ghosts of the other New Market Cadets for their roll call. Then Benjy would know that everything was all right! And anyway, if Fran needed his help to impress this Robert of hers, he really ought to be there to give it to her.

Benjy ducked through his culvert and ran across the field faster than he'd ever run before. He vaulted over the fence and raced down the street to his grandmother's house.

"Miss Leota!" he called as soon as he'd pushed through the side door. "Fran! I'm back!"

Benjy skidded to a stop in the front hall at the foot of the stairs. "Miss Leota!" he called again, desperately. Was he too late?

"Up here!" Fran cried, popping her head out of Miss Leota's place.

Miss Leota came out and frowned at him. "I'm disappointed in you, Benjamin," she said quietly. "I told you to meet me here this morning in order to finish up our little arrangement. I expected you to be here."

Benjy swallowed hard. "I'm really sorry, Miss Leota. I had to go do something before I could come back—it's not too late, is it?"

"Not yet," she said. "Please go upstairs and make yourself presentable."

"Yes, ma'am," he said as he raced up the stairs. He had been so sure he'd been making friends with Miss Leota. Now suddenly she was taking Fran shopping and she was disappointed in him. And Hugh had disappeared. There was nothing easy about this business of having a friend or being a friend.

He dug through his clothes. The best he could find was a clean pair of jeans and a clean shirt with a button-down collar. He washed quickly and pulled on the clean clothes. He slid Hugh's watch deep into his pocket. If only Miss Leota knew about Hugh, then she would have to understand why he was late. But would she believe him? He was sure Fran wouldn't.

"I'm ready," he told them, hurrying down the stairs. "I'm really sorry, Miss Leota."

Miss Leota looked at him closely. "It's quite all right, Benjamin," she said, and she led the way to her car.

Benjy followed unhappily, knowing it wasn't all right. He watched Fran climb into the front seat with his grandmother, then he got in the back alone.

"Look, who is this Hugh whatsisname, anyway?" Fran asked as soon as the car was on the interstate.

"I met him at the battlefield," Benjy said slowly. How much should he tell them? He wanted Miss Leota to understand, to smile at him again with the warmth he'd felt before, not look so sadly disappointed in him. He would be taking a risk telling her about the ghost, but if she believed him, perhaps she would like him again.

"Hugh is from—another time," he explained hesitantly. "He needed me to help him find something that had been lost at the battlefield since the Battle of New Market, and now I've got to get it to VMI for him."

"Are you saying this guy is a ghost or something?" Fran demanded skeptically. Benjy could see Miss Leota watching him through her rearview mirror.

"Yes," he said softly.

"You're crazy!" Fran exploded. "You've finally flipped out completely! Now you're seeing ghosts!"

"Be still, Frances," Miss Leota said. "Benjamin does not strike me as being in the habit of making things up."

Benjy felt relief wash over him. She believed him!

"Does this have anything to do with where you were last night and this morning?" Miss Leota asked him thoughtfully.

Benjy looked up in surprise. She must have noticed he wasn't in his room last night. He wondered for a split second if he was going to get into more trouble for being out in the middle of the night, but then he realized Miss Leota's expression was one of curiosity, with just a hint of a twinkle in her eye.

"It had to be last night, Miss Leota—the battle—" He shook his head, unable to go on. Until he knew if Hugh was all right, he didn't know what the end of his adventure would be.

"Okay, prove it," Fran said, turning around in her seat so she could stare at him. "Show us this thing you claim you found."

Benjy could feel the watch digging into his leg through his jeans pocket. It would be easy to take it out to show them the inscription. Miss Leota believed

him already, he was sure of it. Even Fran would have
to believe him if she saw the watch. But it felt wrong
to him. The watch was between him and Hugh and
Hugh's family. He wanted to share it with them, especially with Miss Leota, but afterward, after he knew
that Hugh was all right. He felt that very strongly, but
he didn't know how to put it into words.

Surprisingly, Miss Leota found the words for him. "I
think this is something Benjamin needs to do for himself," she said firmly. "Perhaps you will show us your
discovery later, Benjamin, after you have done what
you needed to come to VMI to do."

Benjy nodded fervently. "I will, I promise, and I'll
tell you the whole story then."

Miss Leota smiled at him in the mirror. "I'll look
forward to that," she said quietly, and Benjy grinned
back, knowing he had not lost her.

"Just one last thing, Benjy," Fran said. Benjy thought
he could hear a note of genuine curiosity underneath
her obvious skepticism. "What was the name of this
so-called ghost again?"

"McDowell," Benjy told her. "Hugh McDowell. His
first name was William, but his friends call him by his
middle name."

"McDowell," she repeated, turning forward again in
her seat and being careful to smooth her new dress
out. "William Hugh McDowell."

☆ 15 ☆

TIME RUNS OUT

As Miss Leota parked the car she asked Benjy, "What will you do now with your discovery, Benjamin?"

Benjy looked up the curving street that led to Hugh's school. "I'm not sure," he admitted. "I guess the first place to try would be the museum, but I don't know where anything is. Is there a map somewhere?"

"I'll show you," Miss Leota offered.

Fran raced off to find her Robert, but Miss Leota took her time, even though she was already late for her appointment at the library. She and Benjy walked up the narrow drive together, past the cars that were already parked along its sides, and came to a stone gateway marking the boundary of the Institute. Benjy looked around uncertainly. He could see a wide field to his left, stretching across to several towering stone buildings. Those must be Cadet barracks, he reasoned, or maybe where they went to class. He saw a few Cadets strolling along the sidewalks with. parents or girlfriends. Most of the other people wandering around looked like tourists.

"The museum is underneath the chapel, in Jackson Memorial Hall," Miss Leota said, pointing. "Go down to the far end of the parade ground on your right. There's a sign outside."

"Thanks," Benjy said.

"I really must get to the library," Miss Leota told him. "I'm supposed to meet Fran at the monument in front of the chapel afterward. Will you meet us there? Her young man will be joining us if there is time before the ceremony. Otherwise he'll meet us following it."

Benjy nodded. "That's fine, Miss Leota."

"Good luck," she said.

Benjy watched her go. Gathering his courage, he followed her directions to the museum. Would anyone there know how to locate Hugh's family? He wasn't sure how soon the ceremony would start, but he knew he had to hurry if he was going to succeed in freeing Hugh from the battlefield in time to join his comrades.

Benjy ran down the road beside the parade ground, past a row of buildings and monuments. Near the far end of the road there was a huge statue on a tall pedestal, with a cluster of smaller memorials around it, but he didn't take the time to stop and examine it.

Benjy slowly pushed open the heavy doors of Jackson Memorial Hall and tiptoed into the foyer. He blinked his eyes at the sudden cool dimness after the bright sunlight, and jumped to find himself staring at the battle of New Market all over again!

But this time it was a painting. A giant mural hung above the altar, showing the Cadets charging the Yankee cannons. Benjy smiled to himself. How dumb could you get, being scared by a painting after surviving the battle itself! The painting showed the tall Cadet Benjy remembered leading the charge, the one with the white-and-gold banner. But Hugh wasn't there. He had died long before the Cadets charged the cannon.

Benjy turned away uncomfortably. He looked around until he saw a sign that said MUSEUM and had an arrow pointing down some stairs. He felt in his pocket quickly to make sure the watch was still safe and hurried down the stairway.

He found the museum on the lower floor right away, but there were so many tourists milling around in it he couldn't see anyone in charge to ask about the McDowells. He slipped through the crowd and quickly scanned the different exhibits, looking for one about the Cadets at New Market.

There it was! He saw a sign that said VMI IN THE WAR, and beside it was the painting Benjy remembered from the battlefield, the one he had seen that first day he'd met Hugh. Beside the painting was a display case. Benjy sidled past the other people to get a closer look.

In the display case he saw some portraits and maps, and a collection of items that had belonged to some of the Cadets who had fought at New Market. There was a musket and an artillery shell, a revolver, a New Testament, even a well-worn tactics manual that a long-dead Cadet must have studied. But there was nothing in the case that had belonged to Hugh.

On the right side of the case Benjy saw the now-familiar uniform, hung on a hollow stand, looking funny without a Cadet inside. Benjy felt a strange catch in his throat, remembering Hugh struggling to tear open the buttons on his tunic at the battlefield. This uniform was neatly buttoned up, with all its buttons in place.

"The museum will be closing in fifteen minutes," a voice boomed out over a loudspeaker. "Please go upstairs to find your places for the ceremony honoring our brave Cadets who gave their lives at the Battle of New Market. We will reopen following the ceremony."

No! Benjy thought wildly. He had to find out about the McDowells first! He had to find someone, right away. He felt more and more strongly that unless someone knew about the watch before the ceremony, it would be too late for Hugh to participate in the roll call. Benjy scurried to the front of the museum, hoping that the museum director had not already left for the ceremony.

Many of the tourists were trying to make last-minute purchases at the front counter. Benjy could see a man and a woman, both looking rushed and distracted, trying to hurry the customers along. He managed to work his way to the front of the crowd and tried to get the woman's attention.

"Please," he called, "I need to see the museum director, right away! Where is he?"

"What?" The lady peered down until she saw Benjy, squashed between taller customers and the high counter. "The museum director? He's busy now, young man. Come back after the parade. All right?"

"But it's important," Benjy cried. "It's urgent! I have to talk to him right away about the McDowell family!"

"William Hugh McDowell, one of the New Market Cadets, died in the battle," the man working next to her said briskly. "There's a pamphlet about the New Market Cadets in that rack if you need to know something about him."

Benjy realized that the harried man with his sleeves rolled up must be the museum director.

"Please, sir," Benjy said. "I need to know if his family is still living today, and where they are."

"Of course the McDowells are still living," the man said impatiently, counting out change. "Can't you see I'm busy, son? I've got too much to do to delve into family records this minute."

"But this is important, sir," he told the man. He slipped to the side of the counter and reached his hand into his pocket to pull out the watch. "I have to know about the McDowell family, please! Look I've got

something here—if you'll only look you'll understand—
it's about Cadet McDowell!"

"I'll be glad to make an appointment to see you later,"
the man told him without looking up, "but I just haven't
got time to look at anything right now." He handed a
lady a bag with some postcards.

"Those aren't mine," she said impatiently. "I'm trying
to buy this pamphlet."

"I'm sorry," the man said. He hunted around until
he saw the woman who had paid him for the postcards. "Here you are," he said, pushing them into her
hand. "Now let me put that in a bag for you," he started,
turning back to the other lady with his hand outstretched for her pamphlet.

Instead, Benjy shoved Hugh's watch into the open
hand. "Please, just look at it," he pleaded. "This is important!"

The man groaned. "Come on, son, these customers
are important! Look—if it means that much to you,
show it to me after the parade, okay?"

"But after the parade will be too late!" Benjy tried to
tell him, but the man had already pushed the watch
back into his hand without looking at it and had taken
the lady's pamphlet in its place.

Stunned, Benjy let himself be elbowed back from
the counter by another customer. He couldn't believe
this was happening. He'd thought the director would
know what the watch was as soon as he looked at

it, and then everything would be all right. But how was he supposed to make the man pay attention to him?

Benjy could feel tears of frustration welling up behind his eyes. But crying wouldn't do any good! What was he supposed to do? If he'd ever felt like throwing a tantrum and screaming and screaming until everyone stopped ignoring him and paid attention to what he needed, it was now. But Benjy knew screaming wouldn't help. They'd just think he was some crazy little kid and throw him out, and that wouldn't help Hugh. If only Miss Leota were here—he was sure the director would listen to her.

Why couldn't he be taller? Maybe if he were bigger, the man would pay attention to him. Maybe he should try to buy something—did they only pay attention to people who were giving them money? Benjy could see Hugh's face, confident that Benjy would succeed in getting his watch safely where it belonged. Was he going to end up letting Hugh down because the museum director couldn't be bothered with him? After all they had gone through to recover the watch, Benjy couldn't believe it would end that way.

"Excuse me."

Benjy flinched at the unexpected voice. Were they going to try to throw him out so he wouldn't bother them anymore? He looked up warily, determined to stand his ground. He had to find some way to make them listen to him, to make the director look at the watch.

A tall, elderly man was studying him. The man was standing stiffly erect, as though at attention. A ribbon was pinned to his jacket pocket identifying him as a VMI graduate. His thick eyebrows gave him a fierce expression, but his voice had been polite.

"If you'll pardon my impertinence," the man said quietly, "I witnessed your attempts to speak with Mr. Reynolds a few moments ago. Would you permit me to see what you have there? I believe it is some sort of a watch?"

"It is a watch," Benjy told him hotly. "It belonged to one of the Cadets who died at New Market, and I'm trying to find out where his family is now, but he's too busy to care about it!"

"One of the New Market Cadets?" the man asked. He looked surprised and a little dubious.

"That's right," Benjy told him firmly. "McDowell, Private William Hugh McDowell from North Carolina. He got shot before the Corps of Cadets reached the farm buildings, and he hid his watch in a crack between some rocks in the foundation of a shop building there. He was afraid scavengers might steal it, so he hid it to keep it safe, only nobody ever found it and his family thought it was lost. But it was there all these years, waiting."

"I see," the man said slowly. "May I look at it?"

Shy now after his outburst, Benjy handed the elderly

man the watch. The gold seemed less shiny in the indoor lighting, but the watch was still beautiful.

The man opened the clasp and looked at the watch face carefully. He ran one wrinkled finger gently over the old crystal, then touched the stem. "Have you tried winding it?" he asked Benjy softly.

The boy shook his head.

Delicately, the man turned the stem a little ways, then held it up to his ear. His face broke into a delighted smile. "Listen," he said, holding it out to Benjy. The boy leaned forward, and could hear the watch's steady ticking.

"It still works!" he cried, amazed.

The man nodded. He looked back down at the watch with wonder in his eyes.

"Look on the lid," Benjy told him. "That's where the inscription is."

Thoughtfully the man turned his gaze to the watch lid. His eyes widened, and he tilted the watch so that the delicate, ornate script caught the light better. Then he looked back at Benjy and nodded again. "You are quite right, young man," he said, his voice trembling with excitement. "You have something marvelous here."

He closed the watch and handed it back to Benjy. Putting one hand on the boy's shoulder, he maneuvered him over to a door on the far side of the counter. Benjy saw a sign on the door that said No ADMITTANCE: MUSEUM PERSONNEL ONLY.

"Mr. Reynolds," the elderly man said in a commanding voice. "Kindly stop that petty shopkeeping and come here."

The museum director looked up in surprise. He frowned a little, but when he saw the alumni ribbon he left the counter and crossed toward the man and boy waiting for him.

"What can I do for you, sir?" he said to the older man, trying not to sound impatient.

"Colonel Samuel Eldridge Marshall," the old gentleman said crisply, "class of '28. Please take us into your office, Mr. Reynolds. This young man has something you *will* look at."

Dumbfounded, the director opened the door and motioned them into a cluttered office. Benjy followed Colonel Marshall eagerly, still clutching Hugh's watch.

"Mr. Reynolds," Colonel Marshall said firmly, "I want you to take another look at the watch this young man has been trying to show you. I want you to take a very careful look."

"But we're getting ready to close for the parade," Mr. Reynolds began.

"Now," Colonel Marshall said quietly.

Mr. Reynolds sighed and turned to Benjy. "All right," he said tiredly. "Let's see it."

Benjy held it out to him. By now the watch had stopped ticking, but Benjy could still feel how wonderful it was—surely now the director would see for himself!

The man took the watch and opened it, frowning slightly. "It's just an old watch," he muttered.

"Please take a closer look, sir," Benjy said desperately.

Mr. Reynolds leaned forward, resting his elbows on a file cabinet stacked high with loose papers. He looked thoughtfully at the face of the watch, tilting it slightly to study the raised Roman numerals. "It is quite old," he admitted. "Where did you say you'd found it, son?"

"You wouldn't let me say," Benjy told him. "I found it at the New Market battlefield, in a crack in the foundation of the wheelwright shop. It belonged to one of the Cadets who died at the battle, and now I have to find his family."

"Come on, now," Mr. Reynolds began.

"Please look at the inscription, Mr. Reynolds," Colonel Marshall said firmly.

Mr. Reynolds tilted the watch to read the engraving, and Benjy saw him catch his breath in surprise. Before he could speak, a shout startled them.

"Benjy! He's down here somewhere—Benjy, where are you?"

At the sound of Fran's voice Benjy turned around. He saw his sister struggling through the crowd at the front counter, her outstretched hand grasping a Cadet's sleeve.

For an instant the young man in uniform was half hidden behind Fran, and Benjy felt an icy hand squeeze his heart. Hugh? he thought wildly. The figure was built very much like Hugh, short and slender. Then Fran steered the boy through the crowd, and Benjy could see the uniform was modern. But when his eyes met Benjy's, the face of the Cadet was Hugh's.

"Hugh?" He spoke aloud, without realizing it.

Fran led the Cadet into the office, still talking. "Benjy? This is Robert—don't you remember? I told you about him. And when you said Hugh McDowell this morning—well, I know you were just pretending about the other"—Fran made a face at him, still not believing in Benjy's ghost—"but I couldn't help connecting the name. Robert, this is my little brother, Benjy."

"I'm Robert McDowell," the Cadet said, his voice soft and polite. "Why did you call me Hugh? It's an old family name." Then he saw Colonel Marshall, and his eyes widened at the alumni ribbon. He snapped stiffly to attention. "Pardon me, sir, please excuse the intrusion."

Now that the first shock was past, Benjy could see the differences in the face. This wasn't Hugh, but this was definitely the family member Hugh had hoped so desperately he would find. Only Hugh had never expected they would find him at VMI! Benjy felt a surge of delight. Now he understood why he and Hugh had found each other when they did. Robert McDowell and Hugh McDowell's watch had been fated to come together at VMI, and Benjy had been needed to make it happen.

"That is quite all right, Mr. McDowell. Please be at ease," Colonel Marshall said. He turned back to Benjy. "Yes, young man, why did you call Mr. McDowell Hugh?"

"I've seen—his picture," Benjy stammered, "the daguerreotype of William Hugh McDowell, and you look a lot like him." He reached over and took the watch out of Mr. Reynolds's hand. "You said Hugh is a family name—are you related to him?"

Still standing stiffly, Robert McDowell glanced at Colonel Marshall. "If I might, sir?"

The colonel nodded. "Please. I think we are all interested."

Robert relaxed slightly and smiled at Benjy, looking so astonishingly like Hugh that Benjy felt his breath catch. Would he ever see his friend again?

"My great-great-grandfather was his cousin," Robert explained. "I'm the first McDowell to come back to VMI since William, or Hugh, as you called him."

Colonel Marshall smiled at Benjy. "I think this is the missing family member you're looking for, young man."

Benjy held the watch out to Robert. "I found this watch at the battlefield," he said evenly. "It belonged to your cousin. I believe Hugh knew he was dying and hid it to keep it safe from Yankee scavengers if the battle turned against the Confederates. But his family thought he was careless, didn't they? They thought he'd lost it, and they were ashamed of him."

"They were—confused," Robert said delicately. "They honored him for his part in the battle, but, you're right, they were ashamed that he had lost the family watch. When his brother married, he didn't name either of his sons Hugh. But how do you know all this about my distant cousin?"

"Look at the lid," Benjy told Robert. "Read the inscription on the inside."

Robert took the watch and carefully opened it, tilting it to the light to read the inscription. He looked up at Benjy in amazement. "Where did you find this?"

"At the battlefield," Benjy said again. "Hugh hid it in a crack in the foundation of the wheelwright shop. Truly."

"My God," Mr. Reynolds said softly, shaking his head. "I remember now—the Institute correspondence files—the family kept writing letters, asking where their son's gold watch was."

"But it was never recovered," Robert said, looking up, "until now. What are you going to do with it, Benjy?"

"Do with it?" Benjy looked at him, perplexed. "It's not mine. You're a McDowell—you should have it now."

Robert looked at the inscription again. He closed the watch and ran his hands gently over the warm gold. Then he shook his head. "A family watch is a very precious thing, to be passed down to a son or a grandson. It's more than just a way of keeping time—it's a way of respecting family tradition and rewarding family loyalty. I don't think I've earned the right to wear this watch, not the way my cousin earned it."

Colonel Marshall nodded. "Very wise, Mr. McDowell."

Robert smiled at the colonel. Then he looked back to Benjy. "It's up to you, Benjy. You found the watch, and you seem to have some idea of what my cousin wanted done with it. What do you think we should do?"

Benjy had been thinking hard. Hugh had wanted his family to know about the watch so they wouldn't be ashamed of him any longer. But he could understand Robert's feelings—perhaps the knowledge was what needed to be passed on to the McDowell family, not the watch itself. If Hugh's ghost was set free of the battlefield at last, his spirit would come here, to VMI, to join his comrades. Perhaps this was where his watch should be also.

"I think," Benjy said slowly, "as long as Cadet McDowell agrees, Hugh's watch should stay here."

"You mean you want to donate the watch to our collection?" Mr. Reynolds asked, amazed.

Benjy nodded. Out of the corner of his eye he could see Robert nodding his agreement.

"It belongs here," Benjy explained.

Colonel Marshall patted him on the shoulder. "Excellent," he said quietly.

"Do you agree?" Mr. Reynolds asked Robert.

"Yes, sir," Robert said. He stole a quick glance at the wall clock and caught his breath. "Colonel Marshall, gentlemen, please forgive me. I have to be in formation fifteen minutes prior to Adjutant's call, and I've got barely three minutes to make it."

Colonel Marshall smiled. "Then you must go," he said. "Carry on, Mr. McDowell."

Robert whirled around, forgetting Fran in his hurry, and headed up to the chapel.

"Robert?" Fran called, racing up the stairs after him. Benjy grinned, watching her go.

Mr. Reynolds frowned. "The ceremony will be starting in a little while," he said. "We should get this taken care of before it starts."

He fumbled through the clutter on his file cabinets until he found a blank index card, then pulled out a black felt-tip pen from his pocket. "Now what's your proper name, young Ben?"

"Stark, sir," Benjy told him, "Benjamin Stark."

In neat script Mr. Reynolds wrote:

Family watch belonging to
Cadet William Hugh McDowell
Recovered on the battlefield at New Market
by Mr. Benjamin Stark
Donated by Cadet Robert William McDowell

"Will this do for now?" he asked. "I'll get a proper card printed up as soon as possible."

Benjy nodded, his eyes shining. "That's fine, sir," he whispered.

"Well, let's put this where it belongs, then," Mr. Reynolds said. He led the way to the display case Benjy had seen earlier and unlocked it. He rearranged a few things and placed Hugh's watch in the center, propped open with the lid clearly visible so that the inscriptions could be read. He put the donation card beside it.

"Thank you, Mr. Stark," he said.

Benjy grinned at the watch. Now, with the watch safely where it belonged and Robert knowing the truth, everything had to be all right with Hugh!

"Shall we go upstairs for the ceremony?" Colonel Marshal suggested. "Mr. Reynolds?"

The museum director looked around and realized there was still a handful of tourists at the front counter. "I'll just take care of a few of these last people," he murmured. "Then I can close up."

"And Mr. Stark?" Colonel Marshall asked politely, turning to face Benjy. "Or may I call you Benjamin?"

Benjy smiled at the gentleman. "Call me . . ." he stopped for a moment and thought of Hugh. "Please, sir," he said, "call me Ben."

Colonel Marshall nodded. "Thank you, Ben," he said, and led the way to the stairs. Benjy followed him eagerly. Before he left, however, he glanced back at the watch. His left hand closed tightly on the cloth that Hugh had wrapped around it. Now the watch was part of history, but the fragile cloth would always belong to him, as Hugh's friendship did.

☆ 16 ☆

"DIED ON THE FIELD OF HONOR"

"**T**here you are!" Fran cried as Benjy emerged from the chapel. "I was just telling Miss Leota what happened. Robert's meeting us after the ceremony, and he wants to hear all the details. When you said McDowell this morning, I knew there had to be some connection with Robert, but I never thought it was anything like this!"

Benjy grinned at her. "Thanks for finding him, Fran. Things wouldn't have worked out right without him."

"Well, I didn't find him for you," Fran told him. But he thought she looked quite pleased.

Benjy turned toward his grandmother. "Thank you for understanding, even without seeing the watch, Miss Leota," he told her. "I had to try to find Hugh this morning, but I didn't mean to keep you waiting. I'm sorry if you thought I didn't care."

His grandmother smiled at him. "I do understand, Benjamin. And it is all right."

Benjy smiled back at her, knowing that it really was all right now.

He saw Colonel Marshall standing nearby, and hurried to introduce him to his grandmother.

"Miss Leota," he said, "this is Colonel Samuel Eldridge Marshall. He was helping—he made them listen to me! He's a VMI graduate, from the class of 1928. And this is my grandmother, Colonel Marshall, Mrs. Leota Stark. And my sister, Fran," he added, remembering he'd never had a chance to introduce her in the excitement downstairs.

"I am very pleased to meet you, Mrs. Stark," Colonel Marshall said, bowing slightly. "May I say you are fortunate to have such a fine grandson. Ben has given the Institute something very precious today."

Benjy looked down at his feet, blushing slightly.

"Thank you, Colonel Marshall," Miss Leota told him. "And I am grateful for your kindness and for the help you gave"—she paused and looked at Benjy thoughtfully—"you gave Ben."

Benjy grinned at her suddenly. "After the ceremony," he said excitedly, "when we meet Robert, you've got to come down to the museum and see the watch, and I'll tell you the whole story!"

Impulsively he reached out and hugged his grandmother. He felt her stiffen slightly, surprised, and was afraid for a moment that he had offended her. Then her arms encircled him and she hugged him tightly.

"Look, it's starting!" Fran interrupted. "But I can't see Robert yet."

Benjy twisted eagerly to see the parade ground.

He could hear the sound of soldiers marching. He shut his eyes and remembered the Corps of Cadets marching across the wheat field in perfect parade order. Today, however, there would be no cannon fire.

"My youngest grandson is marching today," Colonel Marshall said suddenly. There was pride in the old soldier's voice.

Benjy opened his eyes and craned his neck to see the neat lines of Cadets in their dress uniforms. They marched out through the barracks entrance and crossed the parade ground smartly, then swung to come on line facing toward where Benjy and Fran and Miss Leota and the rest of the people were standing. Benjy could see a space cleared among the crowd where he had earlier noticed the large monument.

Without warning, Benjy felt a strange sensation as he watched the long line of the Cadets march toward him. A sudden chill feeling hit his heart, and a cold finger seemed to crawl up his back and rest at the nape of his neck. Benjy shivered and stared hard at the parade coming toward him, blinking as though he were seeing double. Interspersed between the neat columns of Cadets were other columns of other marchers, weren't there? Rows of other Cadets in familiar uniforms, marching with full battle kit, carrying their muskets proudly.

"They are here in ghostly assemblage,
The men of the Corps long dead,
And our hearts are standing attention
While we wait for their passing tread."

Benjy turned to stare openmouthed at Colonel Marshall, standing behind him. The tall man stood stiffly at attention, softly reciting the words to himself. Did he see the other Corps too? But the old man stood silent now, watching the parade from under his bushy eyebrows, frowning as though he regretted not being able to march beside them. Perhaps, Benjy thought, he was merely remembering the days when he had marched with the Corps himself.

The Cadets turned sharply, marched into position on the parade ground, and stood to attention. The living Cadets seemed shadowy now to Benjy, and he stared hard at the others, the ghosts who had served in battle, proudly answering to their own roll call.

"The long gray line of us stretches
Through the years of a century told
And the last man feels to his marrow
The grip of your far-off hold."

Colonel Marshall's voice, reciting a distant but still clear memory, was soft. Benjy didn't think anyone except him could hear it. He didn't think he would ever forget the words, though—he felt too deeply the grip of the Cadets' far-off hold himself.

He scanned the line of ghostly Cadets, eager to see Hugh again. But there was no sign of his friend. Was Hugh still trapped on the battlefield? Did he believe he would never be free of the dishonor, even now that his watch was safely recovered and his family knew the truth?

The living Cadets in their dress parade called the roll of their past comrades who had lost their lives at the Battle of New Market. Benjy struggled to listen.

"First Sergeant William Henry Cabell," a living voice called out in the time-honored ceremony.

"Died on the field of honor, sir!" another voice answered.

"Corporal Samuel Francis Atwill."

Benjy struggled to shut out the voices of the living ceremony. The ghosts were calling their roll also, company by company—every Cadet who had done his duty on the field at New Market. Benjy could see the ghosts; then, abruptly, he could hear their voices, dusty echoes around the edges of the ceremonial words.

"Woodruff!" called the ghostly adjutant.

"Present for duty, sir!" a voice out of the past answered.

"Yarbrough!"

"Present for duty, sir!"

"A Company all present for duty, sir!"

Benjy thought quickly. Hugh had been in B Company. He scanned the ranks again, desperately. Where was he? B Company had already started calling its roll.

"Private Charles Gay Crockett," the living voices went on with their ceremonial roll call.

"Died on the field of honor, sir!"

"Private Alva Curtis Hartsfield."

Why wasn't Hugh there? Benjy strained to shut out the living voices and concentrate on the roll of B Company.

"Gibson!" the ghostly adjutant continued.

"Present for duty, sir!"

"Grasty!"

"Present for duty, sir!"

McDowell would be coming up soon! Benjy clenched his fists. I got your watch here, Hugh, he thought—I gave it to Robert McDowell and he knows now, but he said he didn't deserve it so we gave it to the museum and they put it on display. Everyone knows you did your duty, they're all proud of you now, even your father's spirit, he has to be. I did what you wanted me to; now don't let me down. You can leave the battlefield now, you can join your classmates!

"Grip hands with us now though we see not,
Grip hands with us, strengthen our hearts,

> *As the long line stiffens and straightens*
> *With the thrill that your presence imparts."*

Colonel Marshall was standing straight and tall, his face proud as he murmured the lines while he watched each Cadet step forward and answer for the men who had died at New Market.

"Private Luther Cary Haynes." The ceremony of the living Cadets intruded on Benjy's awareness. Desperately, he tried to listen to both roll calls at once.

"Died on the field of honor, sir!"

"Private Thomas Garland Jefferson."

"Died on the field of honor, sir!"

"Private Henry Jenner Jones."

Then Benjy saw the empty space in the midst of the ghostly B Company. Why wasn't Hugh in place? Hadn't it been enough to recover the family watch and find Robert McDowell? Hugh couldn't be trapped on the battlefield forever, eternally exiled from the peace and respect his comrades shared. He'd served his country and his family; he'd been true to his honor. He had to be here. They'd call his name any second!

"Lewis!" The ancient voice of the ghost grated on Benjy's nerves. Where was Hugh?

"Present for duty, sir!"

"McCorkle!"

"Present for duty, sir!"

"McDowell!"

The silence roared around Benjy. He wanted to shout "Present!" for his friend; he wanted to run find Hugh wherever he was, hiding on the battlefield, still afraid somehow that he had failed his family and nation— he wanted to do something to show his friend that the disgrace was all past! What did it take? Benjy had defied all his fears to try to help his friend. How could Hugh just throw that away and ignore this roll call?

"McDowell!" the ghostly voice repeated.

"Go on," another voice replied. "He's never here."

There was a dusty sigh. Benjy wanted to stop them, to run out and shake them and tell them that Hugh would be there, he had to make it this time!

"Wait, sir!" a voice rang out. "He's coming!"

"There's McDowell!" someone else called.

"Hurry up, McDowell!" a ghostly voice from the other end of the line shouted.

Benjy turned. There came Hugh, running awkwardly in his haste, clutching his musket in one hand while he frantically struggled to button his tunic. He was panting as he fell into place, but his face was shining. His watch was in the museum display case as a symbol of his dedication to his family and his country, and his spirit was finally free to join his comrades. Now he could allow himself to rest in the peace he deserved.

"Good to see you, McDowell!" someone called as he slipped into the gap in B Company.

"Knew you'd make it," a dusty voice offered.

"About time," the Cadet behind Hugh said, then reached forward and clapped him on the shoulder.

"Good work," the Cadet beside him said.

> *"Grip hands, though it be from the shadows*
> *While we swear as you did of yore*
> *Or living, or dying, to honor*
> *The Corps and the Corps and the Corps."*

Colonel Marshall's voice was gentle now, reverent in honor of the Cadets who had honored the Corps by giving their lives for it at New Market. Benjy felt his own pride as he watched Hugh snap to attention to answer his name in the roll call for the first time in 130 years.

"McDowell!" the ghostly voice rang out again.

"Private William Hugh McDowell," The living ceremony went on.

"Present for duty, sir!" Hugh called.

"Died on the field of honor, sir!" The living Cadet Robert McDowell made the ceremonial response for his distant cousin.

Hugh turned his head as the roll call went on and looked straight at Benjy. His smile of friendship was like the sun breaking out in a darkened sky. Benjy fingered the timeworn scrap of cloth in his pocket and grinned back at Hugh proudly.

We did it, he thought to himself. We did it.

AUTHOR'S NOTE

T his is a work of fiction. Benjy Stark and his family are not real people, and no one has yet met the ghost of one of the New Market Cadets.

However, Cadet McDowell and the other nine Cadets who lost their lives at the Battle of New Market were real people, and the battle they fought in occurred exactly as Benjy learns about it in the beginning of the book and sees for himself in the end. Two-hundred fifty-seven Cadets fought in that battle, some of them as young as fifteen years old. Ten were killed and forty-seven were wounded. Every year, on May 15, the New Market Cadets are honored at VMI in the ceremony that Benjy witnesses.

When I started this book, I wanted to show how the War Between the States was still remembered by Southerners, how the heroes of the War are still respected, and how important family honor was to a Southern family. I worked both with my imagination and through detailed research, and I found myself unexpectedly in the middle of a startling coincidence.

I needed a particular family heirloom that a young Confederate might carry to war and then feel the need to hide before his death. My husband comes from an old Virginian family, and I asked his advice. His suggestion was a family watch. The idea caught my imagination, and a family watch became the ghost's reason for haunting the battlefield. Later I visited the battlefield and discovered the foundation stonework in which he might hide it, and which would later be sealed to prevent his spirit from recovering it. I selected Cadet McDowell from the ten New Market Cadets because of his age, because he was hit by musketry instead of cannon fire, and because he was slain early in the battle before he could come to grips with the enemy.

Then I discovered the watch was real. While researching in the Archives at VMI, I discovered that Cadet McDowell actually had a family watch with him at VMI and that it had disappeared before his family recovered their son's possessions. The family watch my husband and I had imagined had in fact existed and been lost. The letters asking about the watch, which the fictitious museum director mentions in Chapter 15, were actually written by the McDowell family and are still in the VMI files. As far as I know, the watch was never found and returned to the McDowells.

I have no way of knowing if Cadet McDowell might have hidden the watch as I have described. The bodies of many Confederate soldiers were robbed on the battlefield, and by 1864 every soldier knew that was a very real danger as the Yankee army swept through the South. I believe Cadet McDowell was a brave young man who valued his family honor, and I am certain he would have done whatever he thought was necessary in order to keep his watch safe from the invading soldiers.

I have used several verses in this book, which I would like to acknowledge here. "The Soldier's Farewell" was a Southern patriotic song commonly sung during the War Between the States. I came across it in a nineteenth-century collection of ballads compiled by Francis D. Allan and published in Galveston, Texas, in 1874.

"The Corps" was written in 1904 by Bishop H. S. Shipman, chaplain of the United States Military Academy at West Point. Although it is a tribute to the graduates of West Point, it seems to me that it honors the long line of men who have studied to be soldiers and have served their country faithfully, whether they studied in the "VMI of the North" and fought as West Point graduates, or whether they studied at the "West Point of the South" and fought as VMI graduates. These nicknames for the two colleges spring from regional pride and friendly rivalry. Most graduates of VMI prefer not to recognize the Yankee military academy at West Point and refer to the school on the Hudson as the "VMI of the North." In turn, most graduates of West Point prefer not to recognize the Southern military academy in Lexington and refer to the school in Virginia as the "West Point of the South."

Although their graduates sometimes confronted each other on opposite sides during the War Between the States, on many other occasions in our history they have marched shoulder to shoulder in defense of our nation. The rivalry exists, but the mutual respect is unquestionable. Whether on the parade field or in battle, all these man feel the tradition and the high standards of conduct which have been set by previous graduates of their respective schools. I used "The Corps" because I feel it is a fitting tribute to the long tradition of the VMI Corps of Cadets as well as to the West Point Corps of Cadets. I have quoted these lines by permission of the Association of Graduates, United States Military Academy.

I would like to gratefully acknowledge the enthusiastic support of the Virginia Military Institute. I was assisted by Ms. Diane Jacobs in Archives during my initial research. Later, Mr. Keith Gibson of Museum Programs was extremely helpful in securing permission to reproduce the daguerreotype of Cadet McDowell on the jacket of this book.

I would also like to thank the Society of Children's Book Writers, whose 1989 Works-in-Progress grant helped make this book possible.

I would particularly like to thank my editor, Ms. Dawn Butcher. Her enthusiasm and her hard work helped make this book a reality.

Finally, I would like to thank my husband, Lieutenant Colonel Arthur B. Alphin. Although he is a West Point graduate, he comes from a long line of Virginians, many of whom graduated from VMI and Virginia Polytechnic Institute. His military expertise helped me make the Cadets' battle come alive. I would also like to gratefully acknowledge his assistance in providing photographs of the battlefield and the daguerreotype of Cadet McDowell, and his invaluable feedback from his thoughtful and critical readings of my manuscript. And I would like to express my appreciation for his patient and unswerving confidence in me through the years it took to see this book in print.